BURNING ALTARS

A BILL HABERMANN MYSTERY

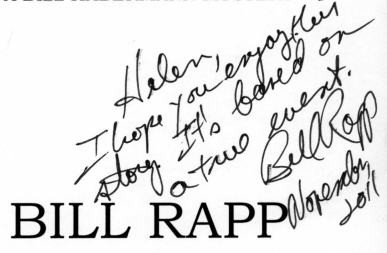

Helen, I hope you enjoy this story. It's based on a true event.
Bill Rapp
November 2011

BILL RAPP

SterlingHouse Publisher, Inc.   **PITTSBURGH, PA**

PEMBERTON

ISBN-10: 1563154315
ISBN-13: 9781563154317
Trade Paperback
© Copyright 2011 Bill Rapp
All Rights Reserved
Library of Congress #2011927019

Requests for information should be addressed to:
SterlingHouse Publisher, Inc.
3468 Babcock Blvd.
Pittsburgh, PA 15237
info@sterlinghousepublisher.com
www.sterlinghousepublisher.com

Pemberton Mysteries
is an imprint of SterlingHouse Publisher, Inc.

Cover Design: Nicole Tibbitt
Interior Design: Nicole Tibbitt

Printed in U.S.A.

ACKNOWLEDGEMENT

Once again, I have to thank all those friends in Naperville, many of whom I have known since my grade school days and who have kept in touch to preserve our friendships and restore my sense of home. You know who you are. Lord knows, I've poached enough from all of you over the years, and it will probably continue. This book, however, is dedicated to my two daughters, Ellie and Julia, who have been a never-ending source of inspiration and joy. I've tried to give you two the kind of life I had growing up in Naperville. I hope your mom and I at least got close.

PROLOGUE

He could've had the damn briefcase if he had just asked or it. I didn't even know what was in it, even though it felt pretty heavy. I had a pretty good guess by then. But no, the creep had to stand there in the doorway, the water from the heavy rain outside on his overcoat dripping onto the floor in a big puddle that everyone would have to step over or into, that sick smile opening his lips so I could see the crooked dirty teeth. Hell, they were just about brown. I don't think he even owned a toothbrush. That's just the sort of man he was. And I knew it, too. When he pulled the coat behind his hip to show me the Colt he had resting in his pants pocket, I guess I just lost it. Goddammit, he must not have seen my own pistol. I had pulled it out of my pocket when I saw his stupid head of black hair march past the window outside. The rain had flattened most of it to his skull and forehead, and I couldn't even see his ears. But I knew he was comin' in to see me. I had that damn briefcase. It sat right next to my leg. The left one. Which was a good thing, since I'm right-handed.

Anyway, when Carl Harbour stepped inside past the cash register I knew it was now or never. So I tipped the barrel up to make sure it would clear the end of the table, and I pulled the damn trigger. Stupid Carl got this big red spot in the middle of his chest where his shirt exploded and a real dumb look on his face. I'd seen that look before when I gave a dollar to the Negro for changing the tire on my car. I'm not much of a mechanic, and I don't like to get my clothes dirty, but I'm a real good shot. Carl Harbour sure knew that now. His knees went all soft, and his legs turned wobbly. He always thought he was too tough for anyone to try anything like that. He looked at me like he was real confused, then just toppled over onto the first table by the door and knocked it and one of the chairs onto their sides. He laid there on his belly, and some of his blood leaked out onto the floor. The tiles were already red and white and pretty scuffed, so it didn't look too bad. I didn't think so, anyway. Although there was a lot more red now than before. Darker, too.

The other customers had all gone real quiet. Stunned, I guess. The shot was so damned loud, it must have shocked them and sent them into some kind of place where you get real silent. But the noise and commotion from the furniture brought them back. A couple of them started crying, and one lady screamed. I thought the girl at the cash register was going to faint, she became so pale. But she didn't. She just looked at me with wide-eyed wonder, and her lips, which looked like long mashed cherries with all that lipstick against her ghost-like skin, just moved up and down without any sound coming out. You'd have thought I was some kind of monster. But they didn't know Carl and what he had done.

I played it pretty cool, even though my stomach was churning inside, and I was afraid I might toss my breakfast of flapjacks. The fresh squeezed orange juice and coffee on top of that didn't help much either. I stood up and strolled to the counter where I asked for a refill on my coffee. Just a little milk to make it muddy brown, please. The way I like it. The waitress didn't say a thing. Her eyes looked right through me when she took my cup and filled it without spilling a drop. I thought it might shake, but it didn't. She was pretty damn cool, too, I guess.

Even though I was nervous as hell and, as I said, my stomach had started to get all knotted up, the coffee helped. It was probably the concentration it took to drink it. I needed to think about where I would go next and what I would do with that briefcase, especially if what I thought was in there really was. First thing, though, I knew I had to get out of Naperville. So that's what I did. There was still plenty of police around because of that church fire, and I figured I'd better scoot real quick. I just hoped none of them had heard the shot. I drove west, out towards Aurora and heading for the Mississippi. I didn't plan to go that far. I didn't actually have a plan. But in any case, there wasn't anyone around to stop me.

CHAPTER ONE

"Well, that's all very interesting." I set the notebook down on my desk. It was one of those old black and white ones with the glue binding, and it nearly cracked as I turned the pages. It reminded me of my early years at school, which brought back memories of the nuns rapping my knuckles, so I quickly pushed the thought out of my mind. There were two of them. The notebooks, I mean. And this brief narrative had been written in a wide, looping hand, which took up about half of the first one.

"I still don't understand what any of this has to do with me," I continued. "Or with anything, for that matter."

Ray Burkhardt shifted his weight forward so that both feet sat even with the floor and his elbows rested on the arms of the chair. He still hadn't taken his raincoat off, despite my invitation to do so when he entered my office. Maybe he was cold, even though he was wearing a red v-neck sweater over a bright plaid shirt and a pair of light corduroy slacks. Our spring had been unusually cool, but it had faded into June, and our daily temperatures now rose to around the mid-to-high 70s.

"You will understand," he replied. "If you read all of it, that is."

"Tell me again why I should."

Rather than answer, he sat back in the chair and crossed his legs, a look of frustration digging wrinkles across his cheeks and forehead. Ray Burkhardt was not a good-looking guy, even in his best moments. Or so I guessed. It's not that I go around evaluating the appeal of men; in fact I'm pretty much indifferent. But his angular body reminded me of the kids we had labeled 'beanpole' in grade school, and his sharp, peaked nose gave him the look of a human vulture. Maybe that's too cruel. But with his long, thin hair combed straight back, it seemed as though he wanted to accentuate the sharp features. So, some kind of bird, at any rate. I was tempted to ask if he kept his coat on to hide his wings. That wouldn't have been a good idea, though, because he looked like he was growing increasingly impatient with my apparent stupidity. Besides, I was not about to pay extra for the heat at this time of year, customer or not. They're not always right, not in my profession.

"Now, look." I leaned forward myself. "You asked me to read these notebooks, and I heard you tell me that they were fascinating. And I'll have to admit that it starts out with a bang, no pun intended. But," I held up the manuscript, "they're obviously pretty old. And the penmanship is worse than mine. I'm not sure my eyes can take all of it. So I need to know exactly why I should bother."

Burkhardt stood up, then strode back and forth in front of my desk, his hands in his pockets and his forearms pushing the raincoat around his rear end, like a long nylon tail. And he kept maneuvering in the space between the rug and the desk, his footsteps echoing over the floorboards. His cheeks puffed in and out, as though he were weighing a variety of words, trying to choose just the right ones. I tried to will him to sit back down.

"I want you to do something for me," he said. "And to do that, you'll need to read those notebooks."

"You said they were your grandfather's, right?"

He stopped pacing long enough to nod.

"Is he still alive?"

The exasperation returned. "Of course not. He passed away back in 1982. He was born in 1890, for God's sake. He died a broken and bitter man. And not just because of the cancer, I might add."

"I'm sorry to hear that."

Burkhardt paused, nodded again, then resumed his walking. "Good. Then you'll help clear his name?"

"Clear him? Of what?"

Burkhardt stopped, turned toward me, then leaned with both hands on the front of my desk. His fingers resembled long, pale talons. Sit, please, I kept thinking. It didn't work.

"You probably don't remember this," he added, the bones of his knuckles protruding, "but Saints Peter and Paul Church was burned to the ground by the Ku Klux Klan in 1922."

"And?"

"And my grandfather was convicted of arson for it. He spent 15 years in Joliet but always swore he was framed."

"What about the murder in this notebook?"

Burkhardt shook his head. "They investigated, but he was never indicted. His water-tight alibi helped."

"Which was?"

"At home with his family."

"Interesting. The witnesses in the diner?"

The head shook some more. "Too upset to get their stories straight. Couldn't get a reasonable identification of the killer."

"How fortunate. But he did commit a crime, so the time wasn't entirely wasted." I pointed to the open page in the notebook. "He even admits it."

Burkhardt stood tall at my desk, his hands resting on his hips and his eyes contemplating contempt. "You might say that. But I'd rather you didn't."

"Okay. Will the notebooks shed light on the fire and the true culprits?" I studied the manuscript with a new reverence. "I take it you want me to use these notebooks as a starting point."

Burkhardt's arms and shoulders shot upwards. A smile appeared, adding some weight to his cheeks. "Now you're gettin' it. I only found them in my parents' attic a little while back when I was cleaning out their house, and I just got down to reading them last week. I was stunned."

"Why not have them published, or take them to a historical society?"

"Screw those guys. They're the ones who have crucified him all these years. Besides, there's some other mysteries here."

I started to page through the notebooks, my interest growing. "Like what?"

"Read 'em. You'll see."

"How about a lawyer?"

"I want to be sure first. And you're cheaper than a lawyer."

At least he was honest. "How can you be so sure?"

His hands fell to his waist. "Alright then, what are your rates?"

I told him. "Plus expenses," I added.

Burkhardt smiled. "I thought so. What kind of expenses?"

"Oh, I suppose in this case it would cover things like a library card."

"They're free."

"Then I'll have to think of something else."

"So you'll do it then?"

"I'll give it some thought." In part, I wanted to reassure him that I actually would consider it. I also wanted him out of my office. It had been a long day with two insurance cases and a deposition on a divorce. "Let me read through the rest of the manuscript first. One thing, though."

"Yeah?"

"Are you Catholic?" I asked. He nodded. "Your grandfather?" More nodding. "Then why would anyone think he'd burn down his own church? Penance too tough? He lose his rosary?"

Burkhardt smiled again, but this time it was a look of triumph. "He was raised a Lutheran but had a deathbed conversion. The family always thought it was remorse for setting the fire."

"And you're telling me it wasn't?"

He turned to go, while one of those boney fingers pointed to the notebooks. "Read for yourself. And we'll talk afterwards. Tell me if you think the man who wrote those words converted out of remorse. The word that kept coming to my mind was 'revenge.'"

"Against whom? And for what?"

He shrugged. "Read on. You'll find a lot of people had good cause." He glanced toward the window. "You having your usual dinner and drinks over at The Lantern?"

It was my turn to shrug. "Probably."

The smile floated back. "Then maybe I'll see you there later."

With that he was gone. I followed about an hour later with the notebooks under my arm and an appetite in my stomach. I figured I'd put away a couple beers and a burger while I read, then finish the relic at home later that evening.

I never did make it home. Not that evening, anyway.

CHAPTER TWO

The Lantern, two blocks and maybe two minutes from my office, was starting to fill up, even though it was only a Wednesday. The bar remained a favorite watering hole for born-and-bred locals like myself, as well as a fair number of the new professionals that had arrived over the last two decades. Naperville had sprouted quite a few good restaurants and comfortable eateries to cater to the town's growing and prosperous clientele, but a lot of the newcomers liked to come to the Lantern anyway. Maybe it was the smoky atmosphere that made your eyes itch, or the smart-ass waitresses who told you to hurry up so they could go home and count their tips.

But I still liked it, and I also liked the Bass Ale they kept on tap. I ordered a pint and a burger to go with it, then grabbed a table at the back, well away from the crush around the bar and the jukebox, but only a short hop from the restrooms. The light from the TV overhead helped. I was hoping not to be disturbed. And it worked. For a while, anyway.

The old man--his name was Jakob Burkhardt--told a pretty interesting story. And it didn't take long to find the real reason for his grandson's interest.

I drove and drove for what seemed like hours. I figured later that must have been around two-and-a-half hours or maybe even three. I was real close to some park, the one with the big rock where some Indians starved themselves rather than surrender to some other Indians. Knowing what those savages did to each other, I figured that was as good a way to go as any. Still, a pretty tough way to die, and I made damn sure nothing like that was going to happen to me. I sure as hell wasn't going to starve myself, not for no bastard like Carl Harbour or the rest of that bunch. And I didn't feel like surrendering neither. Of course, there wasn't no one who was going to surrender to that bastard anymore anyway.

I decided to pull over near the park entrance and see what was inside the suitcase. And boy, was I surprised. When I counted it later I realized I had been carrying around close to half a million dollars in there. I figured out that this must have been a payoff for Harbour, and I knew what for. I had heard all them sirens. That son of a bitch had set fire to the church. The other jerks in the KKK must have hired him to do it. Hell, he might have even been a member of that bunch.

I have to admit, I was just as prejudiced as a lot of people back then, but I couldn't stomach burning a church. What if there had been people in there? Oh sure, they'd probably say they had checked everything out. But you never know. Anyway, I thought they had gone too far this time. No way I was handing this bundle over to that creep or any of his pals.

"So, what do you think?"

I looked up, startled by the sudden interruption. "Jesus, but you've got timing."

Ray Burkhardt still looked like a beanpole. Even more so now that he was dressed up. I blinked twice to make sure my sight hadn't gone bad with the dim light and tobacco smoke. Unfortunately, they hadn't. Ray Burkhardt actually stood before me in a suit. At the Lantern, no less. It was either navy blue or black—kind of hard to tell for certain in the Lantern's evening glow—with a white Oxford dress shirt and a blue and red striped regimental tie, as best I could tell. The raincoat from this afternoon was draped over his left arm. The clothes fit better, but it all seemed to reinforce the boney image he portrayed. He also smelled like a bucket of cologne, English Leather was my guess.

"Are you goin' somewhere, or did you dress up just for me?"

That was supposed to be a joke. You know, just lighten the atmosphere a bit before I accused him of trying to hide his mercenary interests behind a cloak of injured justice.

"Naw." His head rotated from side to side. "I thought I'd stick around here a bit. Check out the action."

"Here? In the Lantern?" I was almost incredulous. "What kind of action?"

"Girls, man. Or don't you like 'em? You're not a homo, are you?"

I closed the notebook and leaned back in my seat. Nobody tries to pick up girls in the Lantern. I think they still have discos or something for that kind of thing. But you'd probably have to drive over to Aurora or closer in to the city to find one. "You ever been here before?"

I knew as soon as the words passed my lips that it had been a stupid question.

"Nope." The rotating stopped, apparently arrested by the sight of a thirtyish blond at the far end of the bar. I leaned forward to see if I knew her.

"I think she's spoken for," I warned.

"We'll see."

Yeah right, I thought. Just then my initial skepticism from our first encounter in my office came rushing back. The bit about his aggrieved sense of justice over his grandfather's alleged mistreatment had gotten me interested. If only slightly. But the revelation about the money and his surreal adventure in search of sex at the Lantern told me this was a case to lose. And fast. This client just didn't seem very trustworthy.

I tugged at Burkhardt's sleeve. At least the suit felt like a wool blend. "I've got some serious doubts about this thing."

He forgot the blond momentarily and fell into a seat at

my table. "What's wrong?"

"Well, in the first place, half-a-million bucks must have been one hell of a lot of money in those days. Hell, it's a lot today. I'm not sure how much that would have been exactly in today's dollars, but I'm figuring at least a couple million. And that's a lot of money for a pyromaniac. Even if it was a Catholic church."

"Have you read the entire thing?"

"Not yet, no."

"Well, he goes on to say that he thinks it also contained a lot of money from some local Klan chapters. This Carl Harbour was supposed to hold onto it."

"To what end?"

"Huh?"

"For what purpose?" I repeated.

"Hell, I don't know. Maybe invest it, or pay for more church burnings. I never got the chance to ask. Carl Harbour died before I was born."

"Why not ask your granddad?"

"Sorry, but I only found this stuff a couple months ago."

"Yeah, you mentioned that already. But what local Klan chapters? Here in the Chicago area? Those guys would've had to have a death wish. This isn't Mississippi, Ray."

"Oh man, what you don't know. The Klan was big here in the north, too. Hell, they were real strong in Indiana. They even had a brawl with the students at Notre Dame in the 1920s."

"But this isn't Indiana, Ray."

"So what? Look it up for yourself."

"I will. And I'll need some kind of test on the paper and the ink, too, to vouch for its authenticity. Or at least its age."

He shook his head. "You won't find nothin' in that. My grandfather wrote all this down shortly before he died. Kind of a last will and testament."

"Is that how you got it? Was this some kind of death-bed confession?"

"Yeah, kind of. He told me where the notebooks were in a letter he left for me to open on my thirtieth birthday. Besides, those tests can be expensive, I don't want you to try to bill me for something like that as part of your expenses."

"I thought you said you recently found them in your parents' attic."

"That's correct. Right where he said they would be, buried in an old trunk. I only recently found the letter. That's why I'm so far behind."

"How old are you?"

"Thirty-eight."

"How do you know Grandpa really wrote this?"

"I've seen his handwriting. It fits, man." The head started rotating again, and the unfortunate image of a vulture returned. "Now, if you'll excuse me.... I'll be in touch."

I wished him luck as he wandered off in the direction of the bar. Fortunately, the blond had disappeared, but there appeared to be plenty of other talent available. The ladies of Naperville had no idea how lucky they were to be out and about on this stellar night.

My burger arrived, and I asked for another Bass. I had gotten pretty hungry waiting for my dinner while trying to think of ways to toss this case, so I momentarily forgot about Ray Burkhardt as I plowed through the half-pound of ground sirloin and the pile of french fries. I thought good riddance when I spied a gray Ford Taurus drive off down Washington Street with someone that looked like Ray Burkhardt alone and lonely at the wheel.

I drove for a long time. In fact, I drove the whole damn night, or most of it. It was around two or three in the morning, pitch black and quiet, and even a bit cold. I know it was June, but the nights were still pretty cool since we hadn't gotten all the way into summer yet. Anyway, I drove west for hours until I got past Ottawa. It took me a while because I drove in circles some, just in case somebody was following me. By then I was so damn tired and my nerves, which had kept me going for a couple hours after all the coffee I drunk at the diner, finally settled. I hadn't wanted to stop because I didn't know who might be following me. But by then I was afraid I'd fall asleep at the wheel.

So I pulled off into that pretty new park where those Indians supposedly starved themselves when they were surrounded on that big rock along the Illinois River. I knew there was some kind of park headquarters there, but I didn't think anyone would be around at that time. And I was right. The place was deserted. Besides, I hoped that if someone was after me, they wouldn't figure me for someone stupid enough to stick around on the state's own territory.

I fell asleep right away. I guess my body was just so tired after all the excitement that it just kind of gave out. But I couldn't have slept for more than a couple hours, because it was the sun that woke me. It was just climbing over the tops of the trees that run all through that park, which probably helped me to sleep a little longer. If it had been the farm fields all around, I would've seen it a lot sooner. The trees probably hid me from anyone chasing me as well.

As you might have guessed, I had to use a toilet pretty bad at that point. So I drove the car a little further into the woods, then climbed out to pee. It was awful pretty in the woods and kind of peaceful with no one around, so I walked for a bit. Then it came to me. I should hide the stuff there, in the park. I didn't think I should keep it there for long. I mean you never know who might find it, even by chance. But until I figured out what I was going to do with it, hell, even what I was going to do myself, it would be the best thing. So that's what I did. And it's still there, or was, at least the last time I checked a few years ago.

That way, those other bastards would never find it. At least it would be a lot harder than if I brought it home with me. Lord knows they sniffed around enough here and even threatened me, especially after I refused to cut that deal that would've kept me out of prison. Screw them. They knew better than to mess with me then or afterwards. They knew what happened to Carl Harbour, and that showed them I wasn't some poor colored guy or Dago they could push around.

I read the notebooks until the crowd, the light (or lack thereof) and the noise got to be too much. Besides, I eventually took the hint that my waitress Angie was giving me with her death-ray eyes that she wanted me to vacate the table so she could get some turnover for the night. I liked Angie a lot. She was one of my favorite people. I liked her open and friendly manner, her short, tousled blond hair and the casual look on her face and in her walk, as though she couldn't care less if you fell in love with her or not. I had even thought about asking her out. Not while she was on duty, of course. I definitely did not want to piss her off.

I drove up Chicago Avenue from the Lantern, a route that took me along the outer edge of the North Central College campus for a few blocks before I swung down Brainard toward Saints Peter and Paul and my flat. Tonight, though, I kept driving. It wasn't that late yet, maybe nine o'clock. I was about a block from my place when the dark, shadowy spires of Peter and Paul loomed ahead of me. The old school stood just to the left with its playground and parking lot. I had ripped several pairs of pants and worn through numerous shoes playing softball in the spring and king-of-the-mountain on snow piles during more recesses than I could count there. Now it all rested peacefully, the ancient battles all forgotten. The original school building next to the playground had housed grades one through five for years;

long ago the junior high kids moved into the newer building kitty corner to the old one, a sleek glass and metal thing that was built sometime in the late 1950s. The grounds between it and the church contained the parish offices and priests' residence.

The blend of old and new, side by side, was something I had given less and less thought to as I became more comfortable with all the changes that had swept over my hometown in the years since I attended that school. But that night the scene struck me as odd, almost tragic. I began to think back to my childhood, so much of it spent running with friends and dodging irate nuns on these very grounds, and the years before that when Naperville had been a sleepy farming community that had made a gradual transition from the German to the English language for most of its citizens sometime in the late nineteenth century. And it had stayed that way until urban growth and prosperity had transformed it again in the 1960s and 70s.

So, I wondered, what had really happened on that awful night in 1922 when the local Catholic Church had burned to the ground? Had the community been the victim of terror? If so, it hadn't stopped the growth of Catholicism here. I mean, that would be a pretty hopeless cause in the Chicago area. Were there remnants of a possible criminal conspiracy still around, a conspiracy that had never been uncovered and never punished? Was there a lot of money to be found? And if so, who might be interested? So far as I knew, only Ray Burkhardt. But had his efforts been inspired by a sense that the funds were suddenly available or in jeopardy? The more I thought about it, the more intriguing it all became. Maybe I could even help right an old wrong committed against a hometown I barely knew anymore. Maybe that would help me reconnect. Maybe, maybe, maybe. I knew I was getting way ahead of myself based on some musings in a notebook that might or might not have been authentic. But I didn't care. I wasn't working on any other cases at the moment. And, dammit, it was my old church and parish. I was even beginning to feel a bit aggrieved myself.

But then there was the issue of Ray Burkhardt. The guy did not come across as the most reliable person in the world. And that reminded me that these notebooks hardly represented reliable or definitive evidence.

Suddenly, I realized I was turning from Naper Boulevard onto Ogden Avenue, the local highway for quick-stop shopping and eating. I drove east, past an array of strip malls and chain restaurants, looking for someplace to catch one last drink for the evening. I remembered the string of bars in the Mexican and Italian eateries that seem to proliferate at Tollroad exits, so I caught a left at Wheaton-Warrenville Road, then changed my mind. Hell, I reasoned, I might as well get that last drink downtown, closer to home.

I took another left onto Diehl Road, which runs past some of the hotel chains that accompany the eateries, like the Courtyard Marriott and Holiday Inn, and a row of industrial plants and warehouses. It's a fairly deserted strip at night, except for those people returning to their rented rooms. It's also pretty dark.

This night, however, I saw a string of rotating red and blue lights ahead, where a couple of Naperville's finest stood around a car they had pulled over. Some poor drunk was about to lose his or her license. Or so I figured.

Then I noticed their attention was focused on a dirt-gray Taurus, just like the one Ray Burkhardt had driven away from the Lantern earlier that evening. And there, looking in the driver's window, was my best friend and local homicide detective, Rick Jamieson.

Slowing to a stop, I got out and ambled toward the Taurus. One of the patrolmen broke free and marched in my direction, one hand on his holster and the other in the air like he hoped to ward off the plague.

"It's all right, Officer. I'm a friend of Detective Jamieson, and I think that car you've stopped might belong to a client of mine. Sort of."

"You his lawyer?"

"Well, no." I tried my most disarming smile here. "I used to be with the force," I said, pointing at his badge, "but now I'm privately employed. I've worked with Rick here often."

"I don't give a shit. Just hold it right there."

"Yeah," Jamieson's voice boomed. "Why should anyone give a damn about your personal history, Bill? This is a crime scene. What are you doing here?"

Jamieson's face emerged from the darkness next to that of the patrolman. It looked like his Saturday night ritual with the family had been rudely interrupted by one of those troublesome telephone calls every cop dreads will prevent him from ever having a normal family life. He had thrown on a gray T-shirt from the University of Illinois over a pair of dirty jeans and top-siders probably in a last second rush to get out the door with no time to change. Maybe he hoped to finish the investigation and still get back in time to finish his Blockbuster or Netflix movie rental with Susan and their son Ricky.

"Sorry, Rick. I parked far enough away, or so I thought, to avoid ruining or threatening anything. But the car looked familiar, and I thought I might know the guy. Figured maybe I could help."

"What guy is that?"

"The one in the car. If you want me to leave, just say so."

"I think you should leave."

"Alright, fuck it then." I turned and started for my car. "That's the last time I try to help the local police as a concerned citizen."

"Bill, that would also have been the first. You know

better than that. If there is any chance you can help here, I'll call."

I didn't answer. I was too pissed. That was the first time I could remember when I'd gotten such a bureaucratic stiff arm from the local law, and it came from my oldest friend. Hell, we had grown up together, ripped our pants together on that playground. I had been the best man at his wedding and was his son's godfather. Then I remembered that I had forgotten Ricky's birthday. I was a week late. Now I was even madder, as much at myself as at Jamieson.

I swung my battered VW Cabrio back onto Diehl Road and intentionally drove past the cops. I slowed enough to get a good look at the car and flip them the bird. What I saw stopped my hand. My heart, too. Or so it seemed.

Ray Burkhardt sat in the driver's seat, his head slumped against the window. Or part of it anyway. I had to drive real slow and look real hard to make sure because there was a lot of blood and brain spattered across the window. There was also a hole at the side where you normally find the ear, and some of the skull at the back appeared to be missing as well. Very big gun, I guessed, and a very dead driver. I knew that for certain.

Ray Burkhardt may have had a funny sense of fashion and some odd playboy fantasies. But I didn't think anyone would kill him for that.

CHAPTER THREE

I couldn't help myself. When I saw Burkhardt's face, or what was left of it, my foot slammed the brake pedal to the floor and my chest rocked against the steering wheel, my head still turned toward the Taurus. I hadn't even had time to put my seatbelt on. Jamieson and his minions wheeled in my direction, and the next thing I saw was my good friend signaling for me to pull over. When I did, his right hand revolved in that universal motion that tells you to roll the damn window down, and fast.

"So, you do know this guy?"

"More like knew, Rick. I don't think he's with us anymore."

"Yeah, yeah. Thanks for the grammar lesson. Were you working for him?"

"Yes and no."

This reply got something that sounded like 'sheeet' as Jamieson grimaced and spat on the road. His hands grabbed the top of the door.

"Goddammit, Bill. I left Susan and Ricky all alone at home with their very own Star Wars movie festival. This was supposed to be my first night with the family in two weeks. So you should be able to figure out real easy how much I want to be here and how happy I am to stand here and listen to you bullshit me about some client."

"Rick, it never got started. He asked me to look into something, but I hadn't decided whether to take it."

"Had he given you a retainer?"

"Nope."

"What was it about?"

"Some family history stuff."

"What about it?"

"That's all I can say at this point."

I knew that would only get me as far as the police station—which it did, incidentally—but I was not about to give up those notebooks until I had a chance to explore a bit further on my own. True, I could've been withholding evidence in a capital crime, and that is not usually a good thing. Especially not if you want to keep your private investigator's license. Or stay out of jail even. But I wasn't sure the notebooks were relevant. Maybe someone had objected to Burkhardt's suit after all.

Anyway, I played the stoic, or agnostic, which got me long stretches by myself in a stuffy, overheated, well-lit room of tile and concrete block at the local police station, broken by intermittent visits from Jamieson and the local police chief, Frank Hardy. Unlike Jamieson, I did not count Hardy as one of my friends. I did not even attend his wedding. In fact, he had suspected for a while that I was sleeping with his wife, which Rick and I were finally able to convince him was not true. I had tried to keep the relationship professional and cordial, but the times he had been trusting, or even civil, to me since I left the force numbered in the single digits. Not that I kept count, but it would have been easy. Jamieson wanted to go home, figuring he had gotten as much out of me as he could, but I suspected that Hardy was enjoying the bit about keeping me there as long as possible and watching my eyelids drop and my head bob as I struggled to stay awake. More than Jamieson, he was dressed for an evening at work, with a pair of khaki slacks and a striped dress shirt. He did leave the tie at home, though. And he didn't even appear to need coffee; his adrenaline was off to the races all by itself.

"Habermann, how come every time a body shows up in this town, you're connected in some way or other?" he asked. I wasn't sure if it was a rhetorical question.

"I wouldn't say every time, Frank. But when it does, it's good for business."

"Okay then, smart ass, how is it good for your business

this time?"

"Well, someone's going to have to find the killer."

Jamieson groaned and turned away. Hardy's face turned bright red. He almost glowed. He was probably so pissed because he realized almost immediately he had walked into that one. Plus, he couldn't hit me. He kicked the chair instead. Then he pushed me over. I think he said, "oops" to show it was an accident.

"You arrogant son-of-a-bitch. You're gonna tell me what your connection is here and how you're gonna help, or they'll be pullin' cold case files outta your ass for a week."

"Does that mean you want me back on the force?"

"No, it means those are the closest things at hand."

"Frank, the guy asked me to check something on his grandfather. Maybe I can help, but I can't do it sitting on my ass here at your station. Let me check into the man's family. You guys can take care of the forensics and all that boring shit."

"What did he want you to investigate about his granddad?"

"Well, he really cared for the guy...."

"Habermann, goddammit...."

Jamieson was shaking his head and waving his arms at me behind Hardy.

"...and thought he had gotten the shaft for when Peter and Paul burned down back in 1922."

"Peter and Paul? What the fuck?" Hardy grabbed a seat at the table, and even Jamieson joined him. "How were you supposed to go about it?"

"I don't know. Check the court records maybe, local press, see if the Church has any documentation still. He claimed to have some additional material as well."

"Like what?"

"I'm not sure. We didn't get very far." Notice how adroitly I avoided mentioning the notebooks specifically.

"Anything else?" Jamieson asked. My best friend could

usually tell when I was being coy. "I mean, that's not your usual line of work, Bill."

"Well, it turns out there's a lot of money in this genealogy stuff nowadays, Rick."

That was a mistake. Just when they were coming over to my side, I pissed both of them off, and they left me there for another hour. My mother was right; I really could be a smart ass sometimes.

Periodically, they returned, and we reviewed Burkhardt's visit, or at least the general thrust of it, which I noted had continued over burgers at the Lantern.

"Any idea why he had been out at Diehl Road?" Rick asked.

"None whatsoever."

"It's by the Tollroad, you know," Hardy added.

"He ended up a bit shy of the entrance ramp," I pointed out when it was my turn to speak. "And there's a shitload of restaurants and bars out there."

Hardy paused for a few heartbeats, studying my face. "It doesn't sound like you guys covered much ground for all that talk," Hardy said.

"Well, he was interested primarily in picking up some chicks."

"And you?" Hardy pressed. "What were you lookin' for?"

"I was looking to get away. I didn't buy his story."

"Why not?"

"Come on, Frank. A church fire eight decades ago?"

"It looks like maybe you were wrong about something, Habermann. Once again."

I stared hard at our chief of police over that one. If he had smiled, I might even have hit him. Luckily, he didn't, and I was able to stay out of jail.

They left again after that, and while they were gone I mulled over Hardy's comment about my quick and apparently superficial judgment on Ray Burkhardt and his case. It didn't help my mood any to realize that for perhaps the first time in his life Hardy may have been right. Eventually Jamieson returned and told me I could leave. He confessed they didn't have anything good enough to hold me on any longer and knew that if I had a lawyer I'd call one.

"I could always call yours."

Jamieson shook his head. "He just does wills and shit."

"He can branch out, can't he?"

"He also knows you. Besides, you'd need somebody more expensive."

He gave me a long hard look, then grabbed the front of my shirt. "I know you're dickin' with us, Bill. There's something good you're not givin' me. You'd better make damn sure it doesn't come back to bite either one of us."

With those words of encouragement echoing in my ears, I walked into a dark night that had suddenly become unseasonable warm and damp. Almost like the South this time of year.

CHAPTER FOUR

It was the kids who woke me up. I crashed as soon as I walked through my back door, but just after eight o'clock I heard laughter and yelling and doors slamming and buses lumbering around corners as Saints Peter and Paul started another school day. Sunlight streamed through my bedroom window, and dust sparkled in the air. Funny how I always forget to close the drapes with the night already as dark as coal.

But it was the sounds of those children that pushed me from the mattress. Did I owe it to them and their families, the few that had been around in 1922, to find out what I could about the fire that destroyed the church? To see if there was anyone out there still connected to the crime, if indeed there had been more than one person involved? A conspiracy of hate? I just couldn't be sure at this point. There was still so little to go on. But I decided that if I wasn't going to do it for them, then I could certainly spend a day learning what I could to satisfy my own curiosity about the church's history and about Ray Burkhardt.

After some yogurt, fruit and about a gallon of coffee, I drove to Naperville's new library downtown, just across the street from the Riverwalk Park along the DuPage River. I had grown up with the library's more sedate—and much smaller—field stone ancestor in the heart of Naperville's miniscule shopping district, right next door to the red brick relic that once passed for a YMCA building. Today, however, we had a much more impressive structure of steel and brown glass to use for our library, three stories tall and admittedly a lot more comfortable and accessible. It also held a helluva lot more books.

The archives of the *Naperville Sun*, our local newspaper, had long since evolved from microfiche to computer, so the relevant issues were easy to find. Sure enough, on the night of June 4, 1922, a fire had broken out in the basement of the church's east wing, just underneath the sacristy and, suspiciously, where it was easiest for the flames to ascend to the steeple and spread throughout the church. By the time the firemen arrived, it was clearly too late to save the building, and, as horrified spectators watched, the church spire slowly tumbled over onto the roof. Damages were estimated at $75,000, while the church's insurance policy covered only $31,000 of that. Obviously, the parishioners had made up the difference. I could attest to that after spending nearly every morning of my elementary and junior high school years attending mass in the new church, not to mention countless Sundays and funerals and weddings as an altar boy.

Nearly a year later the *Sun* carried the story of the trial and conviction of Jakob Burkhardt for setting that fire. He received a 15-year sentence, which the prosecution noted was that light only because no lives were lost. The prosecution's case rested on the testimony of two men, Ralph Adams and--I caught my breath here--Randolph Harbour.

Well, well, I thought. I couldn't say the game was afoot, like the great Sherlock, but it wasn't standing still either. Both men claimed to have heard Burkhardt discussing his plans to burn the church down at a local tavern out of a general hatred for Catholics, and some materials from the church sacristy (vestments, a chalice, candlesticks) were found about a week after the fire in his garage. Both men were also listed as residents of Indiana, where they were rumored to be associated with a chapter of the Klu Klux Klan operating out of the northwestern corner of the state. They had also been given immunity from prosecution, but the *Sun* did not say why.

Now, as a former graduate student in American History, I allegedly knew something about the history of the Klan. And, indeed, while it had originated in the post-Civil War South as a vehicle to fight Reconstruction and the emancipation of the African-American population there, the second decade of the twentieth century saw the KKK expand into the north on a wave of anti-Catholicism and anti-immigrant fervor, with a good dose of anti-Semitism mixed in. Oh, they still hated blacks and all. But having effectively blocked the path of racial equality, the pinheads in drapes had found new people to hate. And waves of new immigrants from southern and eastern Europe brought a host of un-American strangers with funny accents and strange, suspicious allegiances to institutions outside our country. And somethin' had to be done about that there Pope in Rome who wanted to rob Americans of their liberties. And so on and so on.

Sadly, the KKK reached its zenith right next door in Indiana, where it effectively ran the state for much of first half of the 1920s. Ray Burtkhardt had been right about that. True, there were Klaverns, or whatever they were called, in Illinois, but the KKK strength in this state never rivaled that among the Hoosiers. It all came crashing down in 1925, when the local wizard was exposed as a drunken sadist, after a woman he had abused died. Fortunately, she had lived long enough to provide enough evidence to put D.C. Stephensen away for life. And once in jail, he was more than ready to supply additional testimony against his fellow wizards and Kleagles and Klaptrap and whatnot. In fact, that pretty much spelled the end of the Klan in the north, and actually marked the end of the Klan's growth and influence in the Roaring Twenties. By then, of course, the reconstruction of Saints Peter and Paul was nearing its completion. The new church held its first Mass on November 28, 1926, and the High Altar was consecrated the following June.

But in 1922, there were admittedly still plenty of Klansmen in the north, the Midwest even. So I had to admit that the story was plausible. Still, the newspaper reports made no mention of a KKK connection or any money. That didn't mean, of course, that there hadn't been any.

"Geez," I whispered. I was falling further and further into this thing.

At that point I figured I might as well cruise out to Starved Rock, even though I still hadn't found a map for the buried treasure. Besides, I was eager to do something, and I knew Burkhardt's house would be off limits for a while. Before I did that, though, I ran out to the car, grabbed the notebooks and made a couple copies back in the library, which I stuffed under my front seat.

Nowadays, you reach the Park in less than two hours, thanks to the wonders of our modern highways. Route 80 runs right past the Park, which has become a popular spot for camping, fishing, hunting, boating and hiking. There's even a lodge for the pampered and lazy, like me, but I didn't plan on making this an overnight thing.

As soon as I pulled into the parking lot I realized this had been a feckless adventure. Unlike the surrounding countryside, the Park is a forested wonderland with nearly 20 canyons and waterfalls, an array of wildlife and vegetation, and about a dozen hiking trails. I knew this was the case because I read the brochure available at the entrance. The one distinguishing feature, though, was the Park's namesake, Starved Rock. Old man Burkhardt had this right, at least as far as the history goes. According to the official legend, a band of Illiniwek, fighting to avenge the death of Pontiac in the 1760s, had sought refuge atop a 125-foot sandstone butte. Their Ottawa enemies set up a siege and starved the hapless Iliniwek to death. And the Rock is truly an impressive geologic oddity, a natural fortress on the shores of the Illinois River.

But no matter how impressive, it was apparent after an hour of aimless wandering that there was nothing I could do there. Besides, it was already mid-afternoon, and the heat of the early summer sun was making me think of a cool beer and a long nap. So I jumped into the old deep blue Cabrio and retraced my path home along the Interstate, a whole lot more tired but none the wiser.

If I had known what was waiting for me at home, I wouldn't have taken such a long hike through the woods at Starved Rock. Nor would I have stopped for a drink and dinner at a Chili's along the way, although the exercise in the surprising heat at that time of year had made eating seem like a great idea at the time. I sat at the bar with a plate of ribs, pondering the notebook, the Klan and our local church, pouring mineral water down my throat to quench the fire of barbecue sauce and dehydration. I had really wanted a beer, but the road yet traveled and my lack of sleep persuaded me that, in this case at least, it would be best to wait until I reached home to quench that thirst.

But in the end, I didn't get to those beers. At least not right away. It was a little after eight when I got there, and my first impression that something was wrong came when I saw the open door. Now, I may not be the most conscientious person when it comes to housekeeping, but I almost always remember to close the door. Usually lock it, too. Tonight, though, any passerby in the alley behind the house had a peek into the kitchen. And a good view as well, since the light was on.

As I pulled into the garage in the alley behind my building, I cursed the fact that my Baretta was still in the nightstand next to my bed. Or, I hoped it was still there, since that was where I had left it. I tend to keep it there to fend off all the women who want to sleep with me and fail to bring me flowers and chocolates first. But it looked like I was going to have to start carrying it with me in the car, especially when I was on a case. I mean, I had the damn permit and everything.

None-too-pleasant thoughts like these were jumping around inside my head as I snuck up the back stairs, through the door and into the flat. The kitchen is small and open enough to see that no one was waiting for me there. My attention was focused instead on catching the slightest sound from the rest of the apartment, but things were quiet. Really, really quiet. I figured if there was anyone in there, he'd have to come through me, so I grabbed one of the carving knives off the kitchen counter next to the stove and peered into the living room.

I didn't see any villains. Just the drawers pulled from the desk and tossed--along with their contents—on the floor. The chair and sofa cushions had been pulled off their seats as well, and the fabric on the chairs and sofa sliced open at the back. The carpet also lay bundled along the far wall. Crack detective that I am, I quickly assumed that someone had been looking for something.

With the heat rising in my face and my temples pounding, I marched toward the bedroom. I don't know if you've ever had your house broken into, but for me it generated a mixture of intense anger and disgust. I flipped the handle on the knife to get a better grip for a stabbing or swiping motion, then dashed into the bedroom.

Unfortunately, whoever had done this wasn't in there either. But he—or she—had been. The dresser drawers had also been dumped on the floor, along with my underwear, socks and sweaters, and the bed had been stripped. The prick had even slashed the mattress (although he left the box spring alone). Man, I was going to need a lot of duct tape to put this place back together. The Baretta lay on its side in the corner. That, I thought, was odd. What kind of crook leaves a weapon behind?

The bathroom was in much better shape, relatively speaking. The toilet lid was leaning against the wall, but still in one piece. The towels lay in a pile inside the tub, and the medicine cabinet door stood open but the toiletries undisturbed.

It didn't take a whole lot to figure out what the intruder or intruders wanted.

I grabbed the phone on my way out to the car to call Jamieson. He wasn't home, so I tried to control my anger while I talked to his wife Susan. She told me Rick was still at work and made me promise to come to dinner on Sunday. It was a standing ritual, one I truly enjoyed. Susan Jamieson was an excellent cook.

"It's meatloaf again. I know you like that, Bill."

"Will there be lots and lots of mashed potatoes?"

"Of course, if you peel and prepare them."

"Gladly. But this time your husband has to do the dishes. He's really archaic, Sue. See, this is just more evidence that we need that Equal Rights Amendment. And now," I added.

"He says that only people like you need it."

"We'll work on him Sunday."

I finally reached Jamieson at the Station, told him about the break-in and asked him to come over. At this point, I knew I would have to give up the notebooks to explain the turmoil in my apartment. So I grabbed them out of the car, jogged back up the steps and into the kitchen, where I finally popped the Special Export I had been dreaming about for the last two hours.

Jamieson arrived around half an hour later. Unfortunately, he brought Frank Hardy along. They did a quick tour of the mess, then joined me at the kitchen table. Jamieson pulled a couple Exports from the refrigerator, passed one to Hardy, then plopped into the seat next to mine. Hardy stood in the doorway that led into the living room.

"Should we bring the techies in, or have you already touched everything?" Hardy asked.

"Of course I've touched things, Frank," I said. "It's my

fucking house."

"Any idea what they were after?" Jamieson asked.

"Yeah, these." I pushed the notebooks in his direction.

"What are they?"

"Some journals Bukhardt's grandfather kept. Claims there was a big payoff he kept for the 1922 fire, which he hid from those who actually burnt the church down."

"Where?"

"Out at Starved Rock."

"Is that why you were out there earlier today?" Hardy interrupted.

"Jesus, Frank, I'd have thought you guys have better things to do. You know, write parking tickets, harass jaywalkers, catch a killer."

"Well, you seem to have a habit of leading us to them," he noted. He did not sound appreciative.

"Call it professional courtesy."

"You must really want that obstruction rap." He pointed toward the notebooks. "How long you been holdin' on to these?"

"Frank, do you want to discuss the issues surrounding this killing, or do you just wanna be an asshole?"

"Hey, guys," Jamieson broke in, "easy now. Frank, let's give the detective a break for now. He just got his house trashed."

Hardy stayed silent. His eyes would have shot yellow bile if they were capable, right from the red rims, past the straight nose and square jaw. The guy looked like an advertising poster for Soldier of Fortune right now, he was so pissed. Except for the khakis and blazer, which he looked like he'd been wearing since the night of the murder. And his big fat belly, of course. But his face was clearly ready to deal death.

I grunted and turned to Jamieson. "I paged through the thing this morning and decided to run out to the Rock for a look-see before turning them over to you guys."

"Yeah, right." Jamieson did not sound convinced. I was pretty sure Hardy wasn't. But he didn't say anything. "We'll let that one go for now. What do they say?"

"That's pretty much it. There's no clear statement, but the implication is that some character named Harbour set the fire, and old man Burkhardt claims he shot him, presumably out of disgust. Then he drove blindly west until he stopped at Starved Rock out of exhaustion."

"Was the place even a state park then?" Hardy asked.

"Yeah," I said. "I checked on that when I got out there."

"And he hid the money there?" Jamieson resumed.

"That's right. Or so he says in his notes there."

"Any clues as to where?" Hardy asked again, lowering his beer bottle after another pull.

I shifted in his direction. "Sadly, no. At least, not in what I've seen."

"Otherwise, you wouldn't be talking to us right now, would you?" The beer rose again.

I shrugged. "We'll never know. But the local police are not the only ones who have to plan for their retirement, Frank. What with the Republicans in power in Washington, none of us can count on Social Security anymore. You've seen what they're doing to the budget."

"Come on, you guys, can it."

I could tell Jamieson was losing his patience with both of us. "We'll look these over ourselves," he added. "They're all here, right? Or do I even need to ask?"

"Yes, Rick, you've got the whole package. And I have stopped beating my wife."

"Since you don't have one, I'm not so sure that's very reassuring."

"I can tell you what he beats," Hardy interjected.

"I'll let that one pass," I said, "but only to show you both how superior I am. What I really want to talk about is this case."

"What about it?" Hardy stepped up to the table and set the empty beer bottle next to Jamieson's half full one. This reminded me that my own brew was growing warm while we engaged in our witty repartee. I took a long pull and let the beer rinse my throat.

"Well, how far have you guys gotten?" I asked. "Have you looked into the fire and court case? Any suspects?"

"Later, Bill. We haven't had your head start since we didn't know about these." He pointed to the notebooks. "How much stock do you put into this Klan connection?"

I shook my head. "I'm not sure that can lead anywhere. I mean, sure the KKK might have been behind the church fire. But there isn't any Klan today to speak of, at least not around here. There's even a law in Illinois against them."

"That doesn't mean there aren't any survivors of past associations, or sympathizers or relatives of those who were active in the bad old days who are still floating around, Jamieson said. "There's no shortage of hate, even in our enlightened age."

"Yeah, they were really big in Indiana," Hardy threw in. "There probably still are a few around."

"I'd use a different verb. More like 'wallowing around.' Frank's right, though. They were big next door. And there may still be some of those goofballs still there, or their descendents at least. But we can't be certain that the elder Burkhardt actually had some link to them, and that if he did, they're still trying to get that money back. We can't even be certain there was any."

"What's the amount? Does Burkhardt say?"

"About half a million."

Jamieson whistled. "That's a hefty chunk of change, Bill. Even in today's dollars. If they are after it, that would buy a lot of sheets."

"Crosses and kerosene, too," Hardy added.

"We may be getting ahead of ourselves here, fellas. We don't even know there is money still around, or if it's behind this killing."

"That may be true, Bill." Jamieson leaned in real close. "But that gives us something we didn't have before."

"And that is?"

"Motive."

"What about a suspect?"

Jamieson shrugged.

"You guys get anything out of the car?" I asked.

"Yeah," Hardy answered, "a guy was shot and killed. He was definitely dead."

So that's the way it was going to be. Don't call us, we'll call you. Fair enough. They had a right to be angry about the notebooks, since my holding them probably had cost them about a day.

"Later, my friend." Jamieson stood up to go, while Hardy crossed the kitchen floor. "Susan says we'll see you on Sunday. Try not to starve yourself until then. Ricky's a growing boy, and he's less willing to share so much of our food with his godfather these days. Come to think of it, he doesn't like to share it with me either."

"Yeah, Habermann," Hardy added. "Thanks for the notebooks."

"Sure. And thanks for drinking my beer. You guys are always welcome."

"No problem," Hardy said, as he patted me on the shoulder. "And be sure not to touch anything else until the techies get here. It shouldn't be more than a day or two." He actually laughed at his own joke.

"Thanks for the encouragement. I always feel so much better after you guys have visited."

"Sunday, Bill," Jamieson called from the back yard. "Stay out of trouble till then."

I knew that meant he'd fill me in after dinner at his house. But Sunday was still two days away.

CHAPTER FIVE

Two days to assemble my own collection of information on the Burkhardts, and perhaps something on this guy Harbour. Something to use to barter with Jamieson and build a foundation for my own investigation. I hated to rely on the cops; it made me too dependent. And they didn't like to give much away in any case. I figured the best place to start would be the library again. So after I had filled my belly with orange juice, eggs , sausage and muffins the next morning, I marched to the car with a mug full of dark roast. This was going to be a day of serious research, so I wanted to make sure I had the proper nutrition and stimulants.

At Nichols Library I asked the woman behind the information desk to run a Nexus search for press items on the appropriate Burkhardts and Harbours. She promised me those by the end of the day, or the next day, a Saturday, at the latest. That would work, I told her, since I could peruse those while watching the Cubs drop another game behind the Cardinals or whoever was occupying first place. Since it was June, I figured it was about time for the North Side Losers to begin their annual fade.

The local phone book had an address for a Ray Burkhardt, and ironically, it was at this point that I realized how little I knew about my former almost-client. The city directory listed a house owned by him in one of subdivisions that ran along the DuPage River on Edgewater Drive, just across from a park where my friends and I had organized pick-up baseball games in the summers of our junior high school years. In the afternoon, once we were finished, we would ride our bikes to the public swimming hole, a quarry converted in a public works program during Roosevelt's New Deal. There we discovered girls in bikinis and how you were supposed to act like jackasses to get their attention. I recalled that we also played our baseball games downwind from a sewage plant. Not all childhood memories are sweet.

What I found interesting was not that Burkhardt was listed as a bachelor--his behavior at the Lantern had suggested as much--but that the previous owners of his house had been his parents. Young Burkhardt had acquired the place in 1991, so I checked the directory for 1990 and found that Burkhardt's parents had inherited the property from Grandpa Jakob, who had bought the house when it was built in 1956. The directory for that year gave his previous address in the heart of Naperville on Van Buren, a street that runs through one of the oldest neighborhoods just west of the downtown shopping district. There were no directories prior to 1945, when he was still listed as living at that address, which he had owned since 1937. Any further back and I figured I'd be getting his block number at Joliet prison.

Ray Burkhardt's own real estate lineage was not nearly that established or aristocratic. He had purchased a townhouse in one of the developments along Ogden Avenue out by Cress Creek Country Club in 1986. Prior to that he had apparently lived with his parents at the house on Edgewater. And he had sold the townhouse when he presumably inherited the property on Edgewater.

So the Burkhardts appeared to be one happy family with nice real estate holdings in our community. It was time to check things out in person, so I jotted down the addressees so I could go for a drive. I figured I had enough information to get started, and my butt was getting sore sitting in that damn chair.

The first stop was the house on Edgewater. If anything, the street had become more bucolic and prosperous in the years since my baseball exploits, with houses that looked so much larger and trees taller and richer in foliage. The Burkhardt place was a red brick ranch thing that someone had expanded with what appeared to be a Florida room on the southern exposure. From the street I could also see the outlines of a stone patio at the back. And that was about all I was going to see, given the police cruiser parked in front to make sure no unofficial visitors came to call.

So I drove instead to the house on Van Buren. This one was much more to my liking, a two story job of old stone with a large porch that wrapped around two sides of the place, which looked like it had been built in the late nineteenth century. It sat on a corner lot of about half an acre with a two-car garage attached to the north side.

I had no idea what real estate went for back in the 1930s, but I figured this place couldn't have been cheap. Granted, it was the Depression, and Jakob Burkhardt might have been able to get this one for a song if the owner had lost his money in the Stock Market crash or something like that. But what had old man Burkhardt done for a living, especially after he got out of the pen? Did he use some—or all—of the money he had allegedly taken from the Klan? And how would that have looked when he suddenly presented however much cash was needed back then, and all of a sudden? Had he laundered it through a bank somewhere? You had to figure that that sort of thing went on back in those days as well, although the heyday of Prohibition was over. Still, the networks had to have survived for all the other rackets out there. People do insist on continuing to commit their sins.

Maybe a neighbor would know, although I doubted there were any still around who knew the Burkhardts. Not only had a lot of years passed, but this was an area where the construction phenomenon of "tear-downs" was already well established. Basically, well-to-do professionals purchased a property they liked, then tore the old house down and put up a new one according to a design they preferred. And Van Buren looked to have had its share, including the one next door. But around the corner a modest bi-level with a mixture of brick and siding had survived the trend, at least for now.

I parked, then strode up the front walk and knocked. No one was home, so I trotted next door to a narrow two-story number that was covered entirely in gray aluminum siding.

My heart leaped. The old woman who answered the door looked like she had been there at least as long as the Burkhardts. I gave her some crap about doing a series of real estate assessments for an insurance company and tried to bring the conversation around to the house two doors down by telling her how much I admired its style and ability to survive the current redevelopment trends.

"Oh, that one. Yes, it is nice, isn't it? There's actually an interesting story to that house."

I couldn't believe my luck. "Oh really," I replied, trying to suppress my smile.

"Would you like to come in? I could make some lemonade."

I shrugged. "Sure." Then I remembered my fictional calling. "I'm ahead of schedule anyway, and it is getting pretty hot out here."

She turned and shuffled through the living and dining room toward what I assumed was the kitchen. "Good. It won't take anytime at all." Clearly the old lady was eager for company, which was probably hard to come by in a neighborhood that had changed as much as this one, especially by importing so many prosperous and much younger residents. I stood in the doorway, examining the array of photographs and knick-knacks spread throughout a series of cabinets and end tables; all of them looked like solid, well-crafted family heirlooms. The wood had to be cherry or dark-stained oak, and it looked like it could last another couple centuries, regardless of how many tear-downs passed through the area.

The elder woman returned from the kitchen with two tall glasses of lemonade and motioned for me to take a seat on the sofa, opposite her armchair at the far end of the living room. I set the drink on the edge of a white lace thingamajig that grandmothers everywhere use to avoid leaving a wet ring that would stain about a hundred years of craftsmanship. Which was a good thing, since the glass had clouded with sweat, and drips of moisture made small streams down the side. I suddenly realized how thirsty I was. "So, tell me about this unusual history from down the block. What makes it so?" She settled into the cushions and cradled her drink. A loose white dress fell past her knees, where gray stockings ran into brown shoes that began just above the ankle. Clear blue eyes sparkled behind glasses that were as clear as the air.

"Well, there was never anything definite, you know. But I remember how rumors followed the man who first owned the house, at least the one I recall from my years here. He was a manager over at the Kroehler furniture factory by the railroad tracks, fairly high up, I guess. So it made sense to me that he had such a nice place. But others claimed he had made a lot of money during Prohibition."

"And presumably he put that money into the house?"

She nodded. "Yes. People claimed that was how he could afford to keep the property when the Depression hurt sales at the factory."

"What about the man who purchased the property after him?"

She looked confused. "You mean the arsonist? How do you know about him?"

This was where I had to think fast. I sat back against the cushions and waved my hand. "Oh, I came across that when I was researching the property records. It's standard procedure."

She sipped her drink. I followed her example. "What about him?" she asked.

"Well, that's who I thought you meant when you mentioned the unusual history."

Her gaze drifted out the window to the street where sunlight burned streaks on the blacktop. I wondered whether the heat had affected her memories, since it was about a minute before she spoke again.

"I don't recall anything that unusual, other than that the Burkhardts didn't mix much with others. I mean, there was that terrible history with the Catholic church having burned down. People tended to shy away from them, even though the younger ones weren't responsible."

"Was there any talk of where the money might have come from to buy such a nice house?"

She shook her head, then sipped some more lemonade. "Not that I recall. My parents never discussed it."

"Did you ever meet any of the family?"

"Yes. I used to play some with the kids. They were my age. I remember how sad it was when they died in a car crash in the 1980s."

"Do you recall when that was?"

"In the late 1980s, around 1988 or '89. It might even have been a few years after or before that. I don't remember exactly."

"Well. it's not important for my purposes," I lied. "How about the grandfather? Did you ever meet him?"

"You mean the one who had been in prison?" I nodded and drank some more lemonade. "Not really. He didn't go about much that I could tell. He mostly kept to himself. His wife had passed away years before that, and he seemed to be simply a lonely old man who lived entirely for his grandson."

"So, when did he sell this place and move out?"

"I'm not sure. Let me think." She sipped some more lemonade. "No, wait. I think he stayed on by himself here for a number of years after his son married and moved to another place.' She pondered her drink for a moment. "That's right. He stayed here, and his son sold the place after the father died. I always wondered why they didn't settle in and bring young Raymond back here. Maybe the place was too large and had too many memories."

"Do you recall who bought the place? Is it the same family that lives there now?"

"No, the people in there now have only been there for two years. They arrived from Colorado. I never knew the family who purchased it from the Burkhardts. I was away at the time." She smiled. "I haven't lived here all my life, you know. In fact, I just returned eight years ago myself."

Then she stood up, holding her empty glass, as though she was ready to head back to the kitchen for a refill. The smile broadened to sweep away her wrinkles. "Are you sure you work for an insurance company? Those don't sound like the questions some real estate assessor would have."

Hell, I thought, I might as well come clean. I drained my glass, then stood up and pulled out a card.

"I'm afraid you've got me there. Actually I'm a private detective, and I've been asked to investigate the disappearance of some money."

Her eyes grew wide and sparkled with a new curiosity. "It's not the bootlegging fortune, is it?"

"What kind of fortune? Did you say bootlegging?" This was getting good.

Her hands came together in a tight vise-like grip with the soft skin rippling from the pressure. She nodded eagerly. "Yes, that's right. Rumor had it that that was how the older gentleman was able to purchase the house." She smiled with a far-away look. "It added some mystery to our lives here."

"But Prohibition was long gone by then."

Her eyes fixed on my own like a teacher's would on a difficult pupil. It was a look I'd received often on this case. "He could have saved it."

I shrugged. "Tough work in that kind of crowd. Anyways, I'm not aware of anything of that sort. Actually, I'm not allowed to disclose any more."

"Is there a reward?"

I shook my head. "Not in this case, I'm afraid. Sorry." I turned to go. "But if you remember anything else, I'd appreciate it if you'd give me a call. I'll bring the lemonade next time."

The old gal actually laughed at that. "Then why bother if that's all you're going to bring?"

"Alright," I laughed, "you've got a date. And I'll bring a surprise."

I gave her my card, wrote down her name and phone number, then skipped out, glancing at my watch. There was maybe an hour left before closing time at the library, and if my luck continued, I'd have a Nexus collection to read.

And it did. My luck, that is. The librarian had assembled a modest group of newspaper articles that I carried home to study more thoroughly with a couple Special Exports. Actually, the pile was pretty small, only about one beer's worth. So I settled onto my sofa, flipped on the television to catch a Cheers re-run (The Cubs weren't on yet), and started to read.

Aside from a few additional articles on the fire, which added nothing to the story I had gleaned from the *Sun*, there was just one more item on the old Burkhardt guy. It referred to his release from prison in 1937, after serving his full sentence.

Having put in that much time, I figured he must not have cooperated with the authorities. Which probably meant he had something to keep silent about. At that point the Klan had pretty well disintegrated as a force in the northern states, except for some union and strike busting on the excuse that those sorts of things were Communist-inspired. I doubted the feds or even the local authorities would be that interested in hearing what Burkhardt had to say about the KKK's nefarious activities a decade-and-a-half earlier. But what about when he first went to jail? Of course, if you believed young Ray, his grandpappy wouldn't have known anything about the KKK. But he must have consorted with some bad boys if he was carrying their cash around. And like I said, if you're gonna sit for that long, you might as well see to it that you had something waiting for you on the outside that made your patience worth it. Maybe the old lady had a point. I mean, if he had a mysterious source of wealth, a bootlegging fortune would make sense to neighbors who wondered.

Then again, how could he be sure that his bundle would still be around? This really got me musing while Sam and Diane dove into another one of their spats. Did the old man have someone to help or stand in for him while he waited in that cell block? Would he really have trusted Mother Nature to protect that stash that whole time?

The other articles had been selected because they mentioned the Harbours. There was a brief—and I mean brief, just one paragraph—item on the death of this Carl Harbour. According to the press clipping, he was not about to be missed. He had been in and out of trouble with the law, and not just in Indiana but in several Midwestern states as well, including Illinois. Moreover, one of the crimes he had been convicted of was arson, although he hadn't wiped out a church that time, just a barn as part of an insurance scam shortly after he returned from the Western Front in early 1919. He had also been arrested several times for assault and attempted murder, but nothing seemed to stick very long. A real charmer.

Okay, so both articles helped build Burkhardt's credibility.

But there were also two items about this Randolph Harbour from the trial, one on his role in the conviction of the "Naperville arsonist," and another, an obituary on the man who went on to serve two terms as the mayor of a small town in northwestern Indiana. The cause of death was listed as accidental. Apparently his car overturned during a snowstorm, trapping him underneath.

And there were two more pages. These held several items that referred to a newer, younger Harbour. His name was Charlie. That's probably why the search picked it up. Like his ancestor, this one had had some trouble with the law. He had been arrested in the late 1980s and early 1990s for a series of "hate crimes." At least, that's how the newspaper labeled them. These were followed later by several more misdemeanors and some breaking and entering, as well as an assault. Like grandfather (or great grandfather, or whatever), like grandson? I could see the need for a road trip coming.

CHAPTER SIX

The next day, I rose early enough to make that first cup of coffee a memorable—and helpful—one. At first, I wondered why I didn't hear the eager and often plaintive voices of children over at Saints Peter and Paul, but then I remembered it was Saturday. Still, the library was open, or would be by nine o'clock. So I drove there first and requested the records on the Klan's Indiana memberships for the 1920s from the State Historical Society in Indianapolis. It's called a library loan.

"And the reason for this request?"

She wasn't the same librarian who ran the Nexus search for me. I couldn't find her. This one had straight black hair, split down the middle of her head and pulled back behind a set of ears just a tad too large. Of course, if she didn't have those wads of hair pushing at their backs, the ears probably would have looked just fine. Unfortunately, the ears distracted one's attention from the pretty, deep-set hazel eyes. The ankle-length denim skirt and flowered sweater vest didn't make much of a difference, or impact. She struck me as the quintessential librarian. Maybe her name was even Marian.

"Research," I said.

"On what, if I may ask?"

"Of course you may ask. You're the librarian. I'm writing an article on Klan activities in the area in the 1920s."

She actually smiled. Nothing like a little academic prowess to impress a woman. "But why do you need Indiana's records?"

Her curiosity, while admirable as a trait in general, was starting to get a little puzzling. And annoying. I mean, I'm a citizen. I pay my taxes, or most of them. "I want to see if there were any links with the Klan's most successful group in the period. They were right next door, you know."

"Oh sure, I should be able to have them by Tuesday. Perhaps even Monday."

With that chore finished, I struck out on the road for Morristown, Indiana, a small community in the state's northwest corner that once boasted a Randolph Harbour as its mayor in the 1920s. I don't know how often, or how recently, you've driven to the northern side of Indiana, the one nearest our state, but it's a ride I have often considered the ugliest and most unpleasant in America. I once drove along our country's east coast, and the stretch of I-95 that runs from Wilmington, Delaware to Philadelphia can give it some pretty stiff competition, but where Routes 80 and 94 combine just south of Harvey, Illinois, maybe 10 miles east of Joliet, and run uninterrupted for another 30 miles or so past Gary, Indiana probably wins out. The aggravation and despair end only when 94 splits off north into Michigan and 80 becomes the Indiana Turnpike. It's a route marked by a blend of gray skies and brown vegetation, presumably the product of the once-great industrial concentration along the western and southern shores of Lake Michigan. The area includes such luminous points as Hammond, in addition to Gary, Indiana. East Chicago, too. The traffic is heavy, lumbering and relentless. You often find yourself sandwiched between huge tractor trailers, hoping the force of inertia will carry you as far as the Turnpike without getting squished. The roadside scenery consists of drab apartment blocks, one-bedroom bungalows, strip malls and billboards advertising automobile repair shops (no doubt badly needed along this road), and "gentlemen's clubs," all broken intermittently by the occasional tree.

If there was one way to make the drive less pleasant, it would be to slow it down by beginning—but never ending—construction along the entire route. This happened about 10 years ago. Granted, the route is heavily traveled, so it needs repairs and expansion. And the part that has been completed is a vast improvement. But one wonders—especially on those days when you sit for hours on what is, in effect, a parking lot—when it will end.

Having said all this, on that particular Saturday morning it wasn't too bad. It was the weekend, after all. Within an hour I was pulling onto Route 65, the highway that runs the length of Indiana like a spine, which I needed to follow for about 10 miles to the Morristown exit. And what a difference 10 miles can make. There was still plenty of development and traffic underway, evident in the huge shopping centers, hotels and office complexes that surrounded the roads like phantoms of steel and glass. But I actually passed some cornfields. The stalks were about four-to-five feet tall by then and plenty green. That made sense when you considered the wet spring we had had. I also saw alfalfa and soybeans.

Then, suddenly, I was in downtown Morristown, such as it is, with the famous courthouse right in front of me. The ornate two-story building of red brick and limestone reminded me of a cross between a firehouse and a castle. There were towers and turrets set in a square building that covered the better part of a city block. Not only was this building a historic and architectural landmark, but it also had at least one very famous visitor: John Dillinger, the notorious bank robber. He stayed there just weeks before he was gunned down by FBI agents in front of a movie theater in Chicago.

I left my trusty ol' Cabrio in a metered spot by the corner in front of the courthouse and trotted up the steps. My goal was to find out as much as possible about Harbour's life and tenure here, and with all the history around I didn't think I'd have much difficulty digging it out. My first stop was the information desk in a reception office to the right of the front entrance.

A young lad, who looked to be about 18 and the son of

somebody important in one of the offices upstairs, stepped to the counter. His straight brown hair hung over the rim of his forehead and spilled about an inch past the tops of his ears. He looked like he had fought a pretty successful battle with acne over the last few months, and his soft hands suggested Daddy had always gotten him jobs like this one. And in one of them he had apparently learned to smile.

"Can I be of any assistance?"

"Well, I sure hope so." I leaned over the counter and began to flip through a stack of brochures on the town and surrounding environs from the local Chamber of Commerce and county government. "I'm doing research for an article on historical landmarks in small Midwestern towns, and I wondered if there was a book or books I could consult with some history on this one. And the town as well."

"Why yes, of course. Where else have you been?"

"This is my first stop, actually."

"I see." The smile never faltered, not for a moment. "We should be able to get you started."

"I should think so. Didn't John Dillinger escape from the jail here?"

The smile gave way to a look of concern, probably for my ignorance. "Oh, no. That was the local jail, then just a couple blocks from here."

"Well, maybe I can swing by there as well," I suggested.

"Yes, I'm sure you can. It's a fascinating story, you know. He carved a gun from a bar of soap, then covered it in shoe polish to fool the guards."

"I doubt it lasted very long, though."

He looked momentarily confused. "No, but we've had lots of other famous people here, too, and not so dangerous either. Rudi Vali was married here, you know. This used to be known as a marriage capital, you know."

"Why was that?"

"I'm not really sure."

"How about local figures? Any famous or notorious local names? Politicians, crooks, athletes?"

He pulled a pile of pamphlets and a local history off the shelf behind him. "I don't recall any. You might find some in this local history. But I don't know as any would have had anything to do with this building."

"Fair enough." I studied the book, slipped the kid a couple bills, then tucked the tome under my arm. "What about the 1920s and the KKK?"

"What about them?" He got that confused look again. He seemed curious as well, maybe even a little suspicious. I figured I'd better tread carefully.

"Oh, nothing in particular. I recall the Klan as having had a pretty powerful grip in this state and just wondered if they had any kind of influence in local affairs around here."

"I wasn't around then, of course...."

"No, I didn't think so."

"Perhaps I can help."

The woman who spoke those words looked pleasant and smart and very Midwestern. She slid in beside the young man and neatly brushed him aside. She looked like she did this often, and he didn't seem to mind. It obviously beat working. Her short blond hair ended just above the ears, and blue eyes shone with a Hoosier friendliness. If there is such a thing. The white cotton blouse suggested clean living and lots of good hygiene. I decided to speak before my imagination ran completely away with me. "Please do."

"You see, you'll find I know a bit more about the local history than Sean here." She turned to her colleague. "I'll take it from here. Thanks for getting us started, though. I think Miss Klable could use some help sorting the fliers for the summer festival."

Blondie turned her focus and charm on me. "I couldn't help overhearing your interest in our town and its history, but I think the success of the Klu Klux Klan was much more pronounced in the southern part of the state. And Indianapolis was where the real power was. If that's what you're interested in instead of local landmarks, perhaps you should drive down there. It will only take a few hours."

Now, I'm a private detective, so I know a clue when I see one. And this clue pointed to someone even more suspicious and less hospitable than my old buddy Sean.

"No, that's okay. I'll take anything you might have on the history of the building, and then give myself a tour and take some pictures. If that's all right."

"Of course." A hint of a smile crept back across her face as she handed me another set of brochures. I distributed the growing bundle between my jacket pockets. "Make yourself at home," she added. "You'll find we're an open and friendly town."

I thanked her and asked for directions to the library. Then I wandered down the steps to the basement, hoping to find a rear entrance so I could escape to my car and get the hell out of there. I found one, but it was locked, unfortunately. So I ambled through the building, pretending to be interested, for about 30 minutes, then strolled through the front entrance with a smile and nod to my new friends.

The library was a small steel and glass frame job just a couple blocks south of the courthouse that looked something like an elementary school from the 1950s and 1960s. I checked the catalogue for anything they might have on the town and its leaders, but found only one book besides the local history I had purchased at the courthouse for $14.99.

But this one concentrated on the local political institutions, and it contained an appendix on the town's mayors. In alphabetical order. Randolph Harbour had served as mayor from 1924 to 1932, a two-term leader, who retired from political life afterwards to a farm his family once owned south of town.

I drove by the area on my way home. The roads listed as intersections that marked the southern border of the estate were now a virtual beehive of activity that encompassed shopping centers, movie theaters, gas stations, restaurants and office parks. There was even a Sheraton down the road. What did 'once' mean? And how much in the past was that? Had the Harbour family sold the land to developers? If that was so, then I doubted they had anything to complain about. Unless the grandson Charlie had pissed it all away. Or maybe he had grown up to be a jerk all by himself.

This all got me to wondering some more about the local history and whether there might be some useful information on the Harbours and the Klan and whatnot that I could find with a little more effort and digging. I was nearly at the Illinois border and reluctant to waste what had been a smooth and quick trip back. I decided to reverse course and head back to Morristown anyway. Perhaps the nice blonde lady at the Courthouse could help. Or maybe Sean was still around. If not, then maybe they could point me toward someone who would. Besides, if the blonde woman was still there, it would give me an excuse to ask her to dinner. I hadn't noticed a ring, and my social calendar had another one of those frequent gaps for the evening. I figured I had nothing to lose.

The same parking space on the corner was open, so I dropped the Cabrio there and ran back inside. The sun sat low on the horizon, casting an orange glow along an upper rim of deepening shadows, with thin layers of cloud painting velvet streaks across the darkening horizon. It gave me a sense of the night's rich possibilities, but I figured I had to hurry. I probably had about 15 minutes before this lovely Midwestern maiden disappeared from my life forever.

Sean must have gone home for the day, so I figured my luck was holding. That passed, however, when my lady friend's face registered a series of emotions as she saw me, none of them bordering on joy or excitement. Her eyes brightened, then settled into a neutral vanilla when I approached the counter.

"You're back." A nice grasp of the obvious, always a positive beginning. "Did you find the library? I hope you didn't get lost. Morristown is not that large."

"Oh, I found it. Thanks for your help. But I was wondering if I could ask one more favor."

Now she registered some alarm. I was pretty sure the widening in her eyes was not a sign of excitement.

"Well, that depends. We're getting ready to close."

"Oh, that's okay. I was hoping to quiz you some more on the local history. I'll even buy you dinner as payment." I tried on my innocent, puppy-loving face. "By the way, my name is Bill. Bill Habermann."

She smiled. "Alison Peterson. But I'm afraid I can't. I have to be somewhere this evening, and I need to go home to change."

I tried to wave at nothing in particular. "That's okay. How about a cup of coffee?"

She hesitated while the smile disappeared, then returned. "Well, okay, but only for a little while. There's a Starbuck's across the street."

That was fine, of course, since I wouldn't have to move the car. And it was less expensive than a full meal. It took us about 20 minutes to gather our "grandes," since we had to wait for a half dozen clowns to get their lattes with all the crap and production that accompanies those glorified milkshakes. Her look of concern returned when we settled into our seats near the front window.

"You're not going to ask me about the 1920s and the Klu Klux Klan, I hope."

"Actually, I was trying to get beyond the 1920s. Did the local Klan activity die out after that?"

She sipped her coffee, winced as the heat stung her lips, then looked up at me with wide round eyes that settled under blonde bangs shook loose by a Midwestern breeze on the way over from the Courthouse. It had probably ruffled cornstalks and oak leaves around town, and the moment brought a sense of belonging you often find in small American towns. There was a comfort and certainty that surrounded us as we sat sipping our drinks while the sun set over Main Street. I don't know if Alison felt it, but I had to struggle to stay focused on my reason for being there. I guess I was starting to feel my age, along with brief gushes of nostalgia.

"I can't say for sure," she explained, "but there was probably some of it still going on for a little while. Nothing anymore, though. I doubt all those people just went away."

"Do you recall any incidents, any names?"

She shook her head and fingered the rim of her cup. "No, not really. There were some incidents with the integration of the schools and the busing. But nothing more serious than some broken windows. It was certainly a lot less than happened in Boston."

"Was there a large black population in the area?"

She probed the coffee again. From the look on her face, it seemed to have cooled down so I tried my own. It had.

"No, no. There were maybe a handful that had moved here from Gary or Chicago, but they all had enough money to open a business or a practice. I think they were trying to get away from the city as well. A few also came as school teachers. I think that caused the biggest concern for some."

"Why? What happened?"

"Oh, there were some incidents. You know, ugly graffiti, a brick through a window. The kind of blind harassment you get from some people, cowards mostly."

"What about the name of Harbour? Does that mean anything?"

"Sure. It would have to."

55

"Why is that?"

"Well, they were big landowners here. They got into politics but, as I recall, they made their money off the land. I don't remember any details, but I think they lost it in some kind of scandal."

"Were they farmers or something?"

"For a while, but they weren't very good at it, from what I hear. They must have sold out to a developer and made a real killing. It helps to have a shopping center built on your land."

"That big mall down the road."

She nodded as she sipped some more. "That and more. Have you seen all the stuff down there?"

I followed suit, with the sipping and nodding, I mean. "But you said something about a scandal."

Her eyes darted toward the street. "Maybe scandal isn't the right word. But there was some kind of dispute. You'd have to ask someone else, though."

"So, where are they now?"

She shrugged. "I'm not really sure. Rumor has it some wandered off to Florida. I don't know what happened to the others. Some were killed in World War II, and one died in Vietnam. I remember hearing that much. Why do you care?"

"Oh, just general curiosity. The name surfaced in some research I've been doing back home in Naperville."

The coffee cup sank slowly to the table, and her eyes regarded me with a look of dawning wisdom. "The fire. That's what this is about. The church fire back in Illinois. I remember reading about that years ago. Are you writing a book?"

I smiled, shrugged and sipped my coffee all in one innocent gesture. "Something like that. What do you recall reading?"

"Oh, just that some local people were supposedly

involved. There was some big anniversary or something. But nothing came of the accusations. I think they were written off as rumors or innuendo."

"Yeah, and one of those people was a Harbour, who later became mayor. Do you remember reading any other names?"

"I don't even recall that one. What were they supposed to have done?"

"That's what I'm trying to establish. Your former mayor, for one, was an important witness for the prosecution. And his brother was mixed up in it in some way."

"What way?"

I grimaced. "I'm not sure." I pulled on my coffee some more and studied the smooth skin of her face and hands. I had to wonder just how many Midwestern winters that skin had endured and survived.

She must have felt my stare, because Alison paused to study me for a moment before her eyes shifted and focused on people waiting at the counter. Then she glanced out the window. I flattered myself to think she might even be interested in my company. The last rays of sunlight slid off the glass like melting snow. Her smile when she looked at me made me think of other things I'd rather have been doing that evening than driving back across that ugly stretch of highway.

"If you'd really like to know more, perhaps you should ask that man over there."

"Excuse me?"

"Perhaps he knows. Maybe he's even one of them." She grinned at her own joke and pointed toward my parking space. "He's looking over that car with the Illinois license plates. Is that yours?"

The man in question looked over in the direction of the Starbucks just as I jumped up from the table. When I stepped outside, he stood on the other side of the Cabrio, his hand on the passenger door handle, his mouth open, and his eyes locked on mine. Then a second later he bolted and disappeared. Try as I might, I could not remember any distinguishing features from my vantage point across the street. All I had seen was someone of general height and build wearing glasses, a plaid shirt, and a mullet hairstyle. Alison's voice drifted over my shoulder.

"Here,"

I turned. She held my coffee in front of me. "I brought this out for you." Her own coffee rested in her right hand. "It almost looks as though he knew you. It sure looked like he didn't want to talk to you, though. Have you met before? Have you asked him about his family and the Klu Klux Klan as well?"

"Not yet." She still had that grin. "Do you know him?"

Now she frowned. "I can't say as I've seen him before."

"That's too bad."

"How come?" she asked.

"Because I think I'll run into him again."

Her eyes clouded, and she hugged the coffee to her chest. "And why is that?"

"I'm not sure. It's just a feeling I have, mostly from his odd behavior." I studied her face and sipped my coffee. "Odd things keep popping up. Small things, but odd all the same." I didn't tell her about the murder. I didn't consider that small.

"Gosh," was all she said.

I walked Alison to her car behind the Courthouse. We exchanged telephone numbers, then I roamed for several blocks in every direction, cutting a broad perimeter, searching for a sign of the mullet. But the hair and its owner had vanished.

CHAPTER SEVEN

"That's all you got?"

Rick Jamieson suspended the wine bottle about two inches above my glass. We had finished our dinner—the meatloaf was thick and moist and delicious, as usual—and Susan and Ricky Jamieson had wandered off to watch The Simpsons. I was tempted to follow, but I needed to speak with Jamieson alone.

"You'll need to tilt that bottle a little more, Rick, for any wine to come out. I think it has something to do with gravity. Besides, that's an expensive bottle of Syrah I brought, and I want to drink as much as possible before you use it in your cereal tomorrow morning."

"How much did it run you? A fiver?"

"Don't I wish. But as for Burkhardt and the Harbours, I'd say that what I got is plenty. Granted, we're only talking smoke thus far, but there's enough to suggest some real fire somewhere."

Jamieson finally poured more wine. "It seems like you've been doing a lot of running around, with very little to show for it."

"Well, Rick, you guys have the corpse. And, no, I haven't discovered Simon Legree with the murder weapon yet. But you have to admit that there have been some suspicious developments here."

"Like what?" Jamieson filled his own glass, then raised the bottle to show me that it was just under half full. "Some guy with bad hair hanging around your car while you try to get laid?"

I sipped the wine. I had been lucky here at least. The stuff was pretty good. I studied the glass, trying to marshal just what it was I did have. "His behavior was pretty suspicious, Rick."

"How so?"

"By bolting as soon as he caught sight of me, that's how. And what about my apartment? What was that, hyperactive mice?"

"I'll concede there's something there, but couldn't it be related to another one of your cases? Or even one of your many bad dates? Maybe an ex-girlfriend wanted to erase any trace of ever having spent the night at your place."

"You're a real card, Rick, and a true friend. No, there aren't any old enemies or girlfriends hanging around. And what about Burkhardt's parents' suspicious car death?"

"We'll check the records, but my gut feeling, Bill, is that if there was any sign of foul play, it would have been thoroughly investigated."

"Yeah, you're right. You guys never miss a beat, especially when you can pass your first guess off as the only legitimate or rational answer."

"Okay, *touché*. But you have to admit there's little enough for us to go on. Except for those notebooks...."

"Which someone clearly wants."

"So you say."

"You still haven't thanked me for those, by the way," I reminded him.

"Don't hold your breath. Hardy is still steaming."

"He's an asshole. You also have the body of an obviously murdered Burkhardt. What have you guys found out about him?"

It was Jamieson's turn to sip his wine and ponder an answer. In the background, Principle Skinner tried to give one of his moral lessons to Lisa Simpson and Bart. I knew this man. Rick Jamieson, I mean. I had stood at his side during his wedding. We had won and lost God-knows-how-many sixteen-inch softball games on the blacktop playground at Saints Peter and Paul. We had even double-dated in high school and kept a correspondence going throughout my tours in Vietnam. I knew when he was hiding something, and this was one of those times.

"Out with it, Rick."

"Well, we haven't got much. He led a pretty innocuous life here in Naperville. Graduated from North, where he was on the track team and school paper. Attended North Central College and graduated in the standard four years."

"Ever any trouble with the law?"

Jamieson shrugged. "A few curfew violations, one DUI during his college years. Bad luck, mostly."

"No military service, foreign travel, other addresses?"

Jamieson shook his head. "Nope. It seems he was a real homebody. Even lived at home during his college years."

"Oh. Man, I couldn't have survived. No way."

My friend's eyes found mine. They were withdrawn and puzzled, as though he wasn't sure what to say. Krusty the Clown's laugh barked from the living room, and Jamieson snapped back to the present.

"Yeah, me, too. I did find it kind of odd, though, that he didn't have any student loans for his college years."

"That is interesting. Of course, living at home would've helped."

"Yeah, but I'll bet the tuition was still a bitch."

"What's his employment record look like?"

"Straight and narrow. Started out as a bank teller in Downers Grove and moved into the loan department after about five years."

"I'm assuming you talked to people over there." He frowned and gave me a dirty look. "So, what did they say?"

"The predictable. Solid, if boring, colleague. Dated a co-worker on and off for two years, but dropped that about a year ago. No signs of suspicious transfers or transactions. Everyone there was as saddened and clueless as one could expect."

"Anything turn up on the family?"

"Just the car accident you mentioned. Otherwise, the folks were pretty much Middle America and about as interesting as the rest of us."

"What did the father do for a living?"

"Worked as a real estate agent."

"Not the kind of profession that could roll a kid through college all that easily."

"Nope, it ain't. The grandfather's a puzzle as well."

"How so?" I asked.

"We can't account for a lot of his income. I mean, he must have had access to a lot of extra money somehow to afford the house and his son's schooling."

"You mean Ray Burkhardt's dad?"

"Yeah. The old guy sent him back east to Brown. And he probably set something up for the grandkid's education as well. That would explain the loan-free tuition payments."

"What was the old man's profession?"

"He owned a garage and gas station over on Ogden, down towards Lisle." Rick said. "He also had a car dealership for about a decade in the mid-40s through the mid-50s. But I doubt that would have covered his lifestyle. You saw the house they lived in."

"Yeah, but he wouldn't have simply pulled wads of cash from the briefcase. That wouldn't have lasted. I could see how he might use a legitimate business to launder the money."

"If he ever had it. Remember, we haven't established that yet."

"Fair enough. But if he did have it, maybe the old codger invested it," I suggested. "Then it would have accumulated during his time in prison."

"Yeah, maybe. And he could have lost it all in the stock market crash. And he would have had to hide it from his cross-burning friends."

"But you guys haven't been able to establish any other

motive?"

Jamieson shook his head. "Not yet. The kid's finances appear to have been respectable and in good order. No outstanding debt to speak of, not beyond some credit card stuff. There was no mortgage on the house on Edgeworth, however."

"The parents or grandfather could have easily paid that off."

"I suppose so. And the credit card debts were all under $2,000." He glanced at me. "He had two."

"Thanks." I smiled. We did know each other pretty damn well. "So that rules out loansharking, at least at first glance. Any gambling debts, evidence of narcotics involvement?"

"Not that we can find."

"So, what aren't you telling me, Rick? I have this suspicious feeling that there's something else. No other investments or source of income you've come across?"

At precisely this moment, Susan Jamieson returned, Homer having once again proved that he loved his family and the town of Springfield, despite being such a buffoon.

"You guys haven't made much headway on the dishes," Susan said. "What have you been talking about?" She strolled to the counter, retrieved her glass, then poured some wine for herself.

"Easy," Jamieson said. "Bill needs another glass or two to get over the legal limit. Then I can throw his ass in jail, and he won't come around to eat so much of our food."

"Not to worry," I replied. "The cops in this town are easy to bribe. Cheap, too."

"Well, finish it up boys. Ricky needs some math help from one of you two. In case you haven't heard, girls are deficient in that particular area."

"That," I alleged, "is because you don't spend enough of your youths memorizing batting averages and yards per carry."

"Silly us," she said, as she left with the wine bottle.

Jamieson stood up, emptied his glass, then moved toward the sink.

"Well," I asked, "what is it? I get the distinct feeling that there's something else."

He stopped short of the sink. "You didn't hear this from me, but a couple guys have been spotted driving by the Burkhardt place on Edgewater. And one of 'em fits your description of the mullet man."

"You all still keeping a close watch on the place?"

"Not so tight anymore. We've already gotten what we can out of there, but we'll probably go back to regular patrolling to see if these clowns are up to something. Probably not until tomorrow, though."

"And?"

He shrugged. "And I can't remember if we reset the alarm."

"Thanks, Rick. Your turn to wash. I'll dry."

Jamieson was right. There was no cop on watch at the Burkhardt house anymore. The only sentinels were the shadows thrown by the occasional streetlamp or house light across the trees lining the river, all dark and scattered. Slices of black and yellow alternated at odd angles across the water and grass like a broken fence. I parked around the corner on Gartner, then ambled up to the house like I belonged. I even walked around to the back, where I pulled on some gloves and pried out my skeleton key to let myself in. But some cooperative cop or burglar had forgotten to re-lock the back door. He had also forgotten to reset the alarm, just as Jamieson had claimed. I'd have to figure out a way to let Rick know that I didn't need that kind of help. Besides, someone could get in trouble.

I didn't know what exactly I was looking for. Perhaps some lost chapters to the old man's notebook, a map to the hidden treasure, assuming anything was left. Hell, at this point I'd have been happy to come across anything at all. There was a den behind the living room, so I started in there. I sorted through the drawers of a nice oak desk and pushed some papers around that were lying on the top. Then I pulled about 20 books off the shelves to see if there was anything stuffed behind the various Readers Digest condensed books and encyclopedias that lined the walls.

Nothing. I didn't feel like pulling every single volume out unless I really needed to, so I slipped up the stairs to check on the bedrooms. But after half an hour inspecting Burkhardt's underwear and socks in the dressers and the shoes and shirts in the closet I was none the wiser. The shelves held an odd assortment of junk for someone who had never left town, at least to live. But it did look like he had traveled some around the States. There were memorabilia from a variety of National Parks and hallowed amusement halls, like Disneyland and Yellowstone. I wondered why none of it was on display downstairs.

Then I heard what sounded an awful lot like a door opening and closing, then someone walking downstairs. I held my breath, cursing Jamieson for misleading me about his colleagues' schedules. I'd have to think of some excuse without letting on that Jamieson had misled me. I did not want to jeopardize my best contact within the department. He was also my best friend, although that particular sentiment was being tested at the moment. But I forgot all that when I heard what sounded like an argument carried on in a series of whispers and hisses. That, I thought, was some pretty strange behavior for cops. Some furniture was overturned, and I heard a few obscenities tossed back and forth, like "cocksucker" and "son-of-a-bitch." This was followed by a brief wrestling match, a couple of blows, a grunt, then someone falling. Then came a crash of some furniture, a moan that sounded a lot like "shit," followed by another voice saying "goddammit."

I snuck back into the hallway and shuffled as silently as possible toward the stairs. When I peeked around the corner of the landing I saw a human form face down on the floor with an end table on its side right next to it. And the human form was wearing what looked to be a plaid shirt and a mullet hairdo. Damn, I thought. I hope this guy didn't follow me all the way from Indiana.

I crawled down the stairs one step at a time, keeping my eyes and ears alert for an indication as to where the other person might be, presumably the one who had won the wrestling match. I didn't do a very good job, though. As soon as I reached the ground floor a sharp blow crashed against the side of my head, and I fell to my knees. Wincing through tears of pain and a whole lot of anger, I thrust my arm up to protect my head and tried to find my assailant.

"I figured you might be here." The voice echoed like a boom box from the sky.

"Who the hell…?"

There was no answer. Nothing in words. Another blow crashed on the back of my neck, and I stumbled down into a room almost as dark as the one occupied by the body of the stranger next to mine.

When I came to my head was pounding, so I reached up to rub the spot where it was sorest. That's when I felt the wet, sticky sensation that usually means you've been bleeding.

"Take this." Someone tossed a towel on my chest. "It should help stem the bleeding."

I held up the rag Florence Nightingale had given me and found a dish towel in my left hand. Well, in a pinch, I thought to myself. I held the soft cotton fabric to the sore spot, and the pressure actually helped. So did the fact that the towel had been soaked in cold water. Then I searched the room for the intruder and found him seated in an armchair about four feet away. It was tough to get a bead on the character as he sat there in the dark, but it looked as though a dark windbreaker hid an upper body with broad shoulders and thick arms. It also looked like he had dark brown hair of medium length and some scraggly growth around his chin. Most important, though, he cradled a semi-automatic in his lap. In my mind, that meant he had the upper hand.

"You got a hard head. Harder than his, anyway." Mister Mystery pointed with the gun at the figure lying on the floor next to me.

"What happened to him?" I reached toward the body, hoping to check his wrist for a pulse.

"Don't." A rush of breath escaped from the man with the gun. "Just leave him. He's dead."

I looked over at my new nemesis. "And you did this?" He grunted. His bulk assumed a new menace that went a lot further than aggravation. Now I felt more than sore and pissed off. I felt as though I was facing a real threat. My stomach tightened. "Who was he?"

"I think you're familiar with him."

Oh, Jesus, I thought. I rolled to my left to put some more distance between myself and the lump that had never even gotten as close as a casual acquaintance. I still felt sorry for him. "What happened?"

"He got greedy. Like some others."

"For what?"

"What most people are greedy for. Money. Only it isn't his. He thought he had a right to it, but he was wrong. Just like some others. And he got what they did."

"Would that be dead?"

He nodded. "Unfortunately, that's not what I planned. The stupid shit hit his head on the corner of the table. But there's a lesson here for you all the same."

Maybe it was the shock, or maybe it was the lack of sleep. But all of a sudden, anger outweighed the fear. I was a hell of a lot more angry than scared of this callous son-of-a-bitch. "Wait, let me guess. I'm good at these things. Is it, 'Don't get greedy'?"

"You are good. Clever, too. Let's see what else you can learn."

"Can we postpone the lesson? I don't feel so hot right now." I also did not want to spend more time with this sadistic prick. I had no idea what he planned for me, but I doubted it was friendly.

"Sorry." He gestured with the gun for me to stand. "We need to take a ride. I want to talk some more, but you need to see something as well."

"I can't wait." My head started pounding when I stood up, like someone had decided to chisel a new brain for me, from the inside out. "Where are we going?"

"Back to Indiana. But this," --he pulled to towel from my hands-- "we leave here." He tossed it on the floor next to the corpse. "I want some evidence available for your friends that you've been here."

Great, I thought. Jamieson and Hardy were gonna love this one. That is, if I ever saw them again.

CHAPTER EIGHT

And so we went for a ride. "You mind telling me where we're going?"

"You'll see."

Not very forthcoming, obviously. "Well, how about how far?"

He tossed me one of those wry smiles you get from someone who believes he's in total control. He hadn't even tied my hands when we marched out of the Burkhardt house and around the corner to a pale blue Buick LeSabre sitting behind my Cabrio. But he did have a gun sticking into the middle of my back.

"You'll find out soon enough. Just try and make yourself as comfortable as possible, Sherlock."

He didn't even warn me not to try anything "funny," like all the bad guys are supposed to do. With all that time on my hands I studied my captor now that he was standing tall and walking in full stride. He looked to be just a shade over six feet, roughly my height, but I estimated he had about 40 pounds on me. Since he had blindsided me, it was hard to tell if that extra weight was muscle or just extra insulation, the kind that can slow you down. The darkness had fooled me, but in the dim light of an approaching dawn I could see now that he wore a crewcut with long sideburns that ran past his ears and about two days of stubble that swept across puffy cheeks and a square jaw that looked set for trouble. Maybe it was the scar that jutted along the side of his chin for about three inches that gave him an air of rough experience. I felt the soft wound along the side of my forehead and hoped I'd have the chance to find out just how experienced he was.

At least he didn't take the interstate. Instead, we rode south from Naperville along Route 53, past suburbia and even Joliet, until we began to see the kinds of farmland that used to be a common sight when I was growing up around here: open fields that stretched across the Midwestern plains, broken only by occasional patches of forest, brown fence posts, and rusted wire. I thought of old man Burkhardt and how all this must have looked to him when he drove this territory on that fateful night. After all, he was the reason I was in this mess, ultimately.

That also got me thinking about the case, such as it was, and my predicament. There was the body, of course, and the absence of an alternative motive to the story young Ray Burkhardt had woven around these notebooks. And, as I had explained to Rick Jamieson, someone had obviously thought I had something he or she wanted. What else could that be, and if so, why were they so precious?

I glanced over at my chauffeur, the asshole. The smile was still there. But just what did he have to do with all this? My guess was that he was probably the one behind the ransacking of my flat. He was certainly the most obvious candidate. It was good thing he hadn't thought to search my car, if he knew which one it was, that is. Maybe he wasn't so clever after all. And then I got to thinking about my good friend Rick Jamieson. Just why had he led me to that house? Could he have known there would be other visitors? He was the one who mentioned the strangers cruising the neighborhood. But why lead me right to them? That was a hard thing to swallow coming, as it did, from someone who shared as much history with me as just about anyone in the world. What had he hoped I'd find? Hadn't the cops done a thorough job themselves inspecting the place? Only, I suddenly realized, if they knew what they were looking for. So I was either the bait or the ferret.

Somewhere around Kankakee we turned east, aiming for the low and jagged ridge of orange that was opening on the horizon against a sky of slate. By the time we started driving north, just a short while after we passed a sign welcoming us to Indiana, rays of bright yellow were beginning to peek around the barns and over the top of a green carpet of foliage. Things were falling into place.

When we pulled into a wide gravel driveway that ran from a barn to a dirty white farmhouse the day had arrived in all its glory. The house looked like it hadn't seen a fresh coat of paint since the last time the Klan was a force in this state, back during the Harding administration. The barn, too. All it needed was an ad for chewing tobacco posted on its side and the place would have made a great poster. A rusted tractor from around the time the building had last seen some paint and carpentry work sat parked next to the silo. There wasn't even any rubber on the wheels. But there were two very contemporary cars over by the rear entrance to the house: a Toyota Corolla and an SUV, an Explorer, I guessed. They all looked the same to me.

"It was you, wasn't it?" I asked.

"What?"

"The one who broke into my place, looking for whatever."

"You're a curious guy."

"It goes with the work. I'm also curious about the dead guy you left back in Naperville."

He didn't say a thing. The son-of-a-bitch just rolled out of the car and ambled up to the rear door. Unfortunately, he took the keys with him. And that damn smile. I had forgotten the fear factor. I just really disliked him now.

Since I didn't see any keys in the other cars, I walked into the house and followed the sounds of his footsteps through a kitchen that, for the most part, matched the paint jobs outside. The place did have some modern appliances, circa 1970 maybe. An Amana refrigerator-freezer and a Westinghouse stove and oven. A Mr. Coffee sat next to a double sink with about six cups still in the pot. I found a nearly clean mug in a cupboard above the coffeemaker, poured some slop (it looked like someone had brewed the stuff before we left Naperville), then found my escort sitting in the living room with two women.

He shared the sofa with a hefty number, one you could describe charitably as 'big-boned.' She actually seemed to fit the description, because she didn't appear to be carrying a lot of excess flab. Her light brown hair had been trimmed short, and she wore a long-sleeved T-shirt that fell over a couple of very large breasts and settled in a lap bordered by faded blue jeans. An advertisement for a local hardware store on the front of the shirt rode over and down through a bumpy cleavage, but I never did get the entire address. She regarded me with a mixture of contempt and suspicion. I hoped maybe it was because I came from Illinois. I had dealt with Hoosiers before.

The other woman weighed about 50 pounds less and wore her black hair in a long braid that extended midway down her spine. She, too, wore a long-sleeve T-shirt that ran to the end of her butt, which was also encased in a pair of faded blue jeans that she seemed to have poured over her rear and thighs. And they looked like nice ones, too. Her shirt front was blank, but I peeked anyway. She also had a thin nose and deep-set eyes that were more sharply defined than the other woman's. She was very nice to look at. At the time, however, I didn't really have romance on my mind.

"So, what's this?" I asked. "A Harbour family reunion? This what the mayor retired to? This all that's left of the family estate?"

They all smiled this time and looked at each other, as if they were sharing some secret.

"I see you found the coffee." This came from the thin one, who rose from an armchair and walked toward the kitchen.

"And helped yourself." The hefty one spat those words like she had found something unpleasant on her tongue.

Probably came from the coffee.

"Well, I earned it."

"You want some sugar or cream?" Ms. Thin asked from the kitchen.

"No, thanks. I'll stick to just straight tar this morning." I took a sip and gasped from the powerful taste packed into eight ounces of liquid caffeine. Hell, who needed sleep with this stuff around, I thought. "Let's get down to business. Just what the fuck am I doing here?" I was starting to lose my patience all over again. And lack of sleep makes me cranky at my age, regardless of how much caffeine I ingest. I sipped some more coffee anyway.

Finally, the big guy's smile disappeared. He picked his partner's hand up from the sofa cushion and leaned forward. "You've guessed, at least, that we're family here. I'm not going to tell you anymore about us than that. If you're such a great detective, Sherlock, you'll figure it out. But you've probably guessed as well that we are interested in the Burkhardt package."

"Oh man, it's too early for riddles. Just what the hell package are you talking about?" I sipped more coffee. God, it really was awful. I tried to grimace enough to get them to make a fresh pot. I hoped my intestines would survive. Mrs. Hefty just smiled.

"I believe you know exactly what I'm referring to, so don't play stupid. We're all too smart here for that. And that includes you. The best thing you can do is give up Burkhardt's journal."

"I don't have it. And even if I did, why should I pass it to you?"

"Because it belongs to us. It involves property that was stolen from its rightful owners."

"Oh, shit. The Klan? Give me a fuckin' break."

Mrs. Hefty's lips curled. I suddenly had the image of an attack dog, something big and muscular, like a Rottweiler.

Then a set of thin, feminine fingers reached down and grabbed my ears by the lobe and started to twist. Now, normally I'm all for that kind of foreplay. But this was painful. The grip was as solid as a vice, and the pressure increased bit by bit until I could have sworn the ear was horizontal. Then a quiet, very lady-like voice spoke words that should have been comforting, or enticing. But they weren't.

"There are ladies present. So I'm going to ask you just this once to watch your language."

Ms. Skinny had moved back into the room and slid behind my chair without a sound. My ear had passed five o'clock in its rotation before I realized it was her. She clearly moved with a stealth and speed that I was going to have to remember. I also noticed that I had spilled some of the coffee in my lap. This was no great loss as far as the coffee was concerned, but it was pretty damn hot.

"Okay, okay. I'm sorry. Let go, will ya?"

She did. I rubbed my ear and glanced around at this woman. Black eyes the color of night considered me, but I wasn't sure for what. In fact, the longer we stared at each other, the more those eyes came to remind me of something deep and dark and a whole lot more mysterious than any hole I had ever looked into. It was almost theological. Maybe it was death. Maybe it was sex. But it was definitely scary. I drank some more coffee and didn't even mind the taste anymore. I turned back to the couple on the sofa.

"The money's probably gone anyway. I mean, gee whiz…." I shot a glance at Ms. Dark Eyes. "How long do you expect a couple hundred thousand dollars to last nowadays, anyway?"

The man dropped his partner's hand and sat back into the cushions. "You know," he said, "I expected more from someone Ray Burkhardt had trusted enough to bring into this issue, from someone who had the courage and curiosity to pursue leads back to the various properties the Burkhardts had purchased with stolen goods."

"Well, if the money was stolen, it should go back to your buddies so they can buy some more sheets."

The smile returned, and he shook his head, "The money would be nice, and once it's back we will dispose of it properly. But that isn't the only thing. Jakob Burkhardt stole something much more valuable."

"Your pride?"

My mother had often said that I was too much of a smart ass for my own good. This may have been one of those times. The big guy's smile melted, and he jumped from the couch with a speed that suggested his weight wasn't all fat. Hardly any of it, as a matter of fact. His hands gripped the front of my shirt and slammed me against the back of the chair three times with a power and velocity that told me he was pretty damn strong, too. I filed that away for future reference. Meanwhile, the rest of the coffee spread in a deepening brown stain across the carpet.

"Listen, you cocksucker. You know goddamn well what I mean. After all these years I'm not going to keep playin' games with a shithead like you. And you know damn well what I want. If not, I'd suggest you get your ass in gear enough to find out."

I balled my fist and calculated the time it would take for it to travel from my lap to his groin. "Why should I?"

"Because it could save your life." He released my shirt front and straightened himself.

"Does that include expenses?"

The smile drifted back. "You're quite the comic for someone who nearly followed the Burkhardts to his rewards on high."

"Is that what happened to the other guy?"

"Charlie got greedy, as I said."

"Charlie?"

"That's right. Charlie Harbour. He had gotten to be a problem. Too much of one, in fact." He stared at me with a set jaw and hard eyes. "It wasn't supposed to go down like that, but what's done is done. We'll be just fine without him."

"Who said so?" I pressed. "The Klan, or what's left of it? I paused. "And just who are you guys, anyway?"

He turned and held out his hand to Mrs. Big Bones. "Come on, Mary. It's been a long night, and I need some sleep." His gaze returned to me. "You may be interested to know that what happened back there was a mistake. But it shows what can happen when I lose my temper. And I don't want to make anymore mistakes before I get what I need from you. That's why I'm going to leave you to think about what I said."

They started toward the stairs, then stopped. "Sheila, please see to Mr. Habermann. He's a long way from home."

Sheila stepped between me and the stairs while the other two ascended. "You need anything?"

"Yeah. How about a ride home?" She smiled at that. "Do you have a job? Just drop me off on your way to work."

She walked toward the kitchen and threw a glance at the ceiling. Perhaps it was my imagination, but she seemed to hesitate for just a moment. "Sorry. My shift at Movievideos doesn't start until later this afternoon. How about some more coffee?"

I studied the inside of my mug, which was stained the color of top soil. I followed her into the kitchen, where I handed the mug over. "No thanks. Unless you're brewing some fresh stuff." I waited about 10 seconds. "A name would be nice, too."

"You heard it already. It's Sheila."

"I mean a family name."

"I'll see what I can do." She grabbed the decanter and emptied what was left of the coffee into the sink. I said a prayer for the plumbing. "About the coffee." Then she set the decanter back on the hot plate, pulled a filter from under the sink, set it in the cone and began to scoop fresh grounds of Folgers into the top of Mr. Coffee.

"So, you're okay with being an accessory to murder." I figured I'd go at her directly. It wasn't like I had a whole lot of time.

"He's not gonna kill you." Her words drifted over her shoulder while she finished with the coffee. "At least not yet. And especially if you're not gonna cross him."

"I wasn't talking about me."

She flipped the switch on the coffeemaker, turned toward me, and rested her rear against the counter. It was the first time in my life I've envied linoleum. She stayed silent, but those eyes worked their way right through me. I tried to stare her down but lost the match. I glanced out the window. An old kitchen radio the size of a handbag was playing the kind of music my parents had listened to. A clear female voice sang "Fly Me to the Moon" with a strong trumpet in the background like it was trying to put the music in orbit. The world outside did not resemble a moonscape, though, just a meadow rich with green corn stalks that flowed under a wind that seemed to come from somewhere in the past.

"What about this Charlie guy? You okay with that? And do you know what happened to Ray Burkhardt?"

She paused for a moment, as though she needed to consider this new wrinkle. Her eyes stayed focused on her feet for a while before she looked back up at me. "I don't know anything about those people."

"Well, I do. I found their bodies back in Naperville."

She shuffled her weight from one foot to the other. "I got nothin' to do with that."

"You do now. It's called being an accessory after the

77

fact."

Her gaze darted back toward the floor and stayed there. She also crossed her arms and gave herself a hug to ward off what looked like a good-sized shiver. Her tough gal act was a lot less convincing right now. I decided to try a different approach. "Then give me a ride back. At least get me where I can catch a bus or a train or something."

Footsteps pushed across floorboards above us. A door slammed. Her eyes followed every sound. "What are you gonna do when you get back?"

"I'm not sure yet." She gazed at me with eyes a lot more troubled now. "There's still a lot to figure out before I take my next steps."

"Like what?"

"Like how all this ties together. There are several loose ends, including the role of Mr. Big upstairs, the local police, the Burkhardt family. And that's just for starters."

"You think you can get to the bottom of this? You really want to?"

"Yes, I do. It's the way I'm wired."

"You don't have your own agenda here?" she asked. "You ain't in it just for the money?"

"I told you, I don't think there is any money. Not anymore."

"Then why go into it?"

I thought about the killings, but she now knew about those, although I wasn't sure just how much she knew. "A man came to me with a story. It sounded like a crock. So I blew him off. Now he's dead."

"You think you could've fixed that? You think you're that special?"

"I don't know about that, but it might have gone differently if I hadn't been so full of myself. In any case, I still have to find out what happened."

Those deep, dark eyes studied me some more. Coffee

spilled into the glass pot, and steam seeped from the edges of the filter. Sunlight splashed against the windowpane and sliced the gray air around us. Through it all her eyes never moved.

"And your buddy up there" --I pointed at the ceiling-- "got me in even deeper when he brought me here."

"How do I know you won't just run to the police?"

"I will have to go there, eventually. But I need to figure out how all this fits together, and I don't exactly trust them either." I paused to catch her gaze when she raised it from the floor. "I can speak up for you then. I can tell them you had no part in the killings."

She glanced in the direction of the bedroom upstairs again, then stared out the window. "I didn't, anyways."

"So, who is he?" I asked. "Your Grand Poobah?"

She turned her face toward me. "No, he's my brother."

"He got a name?"

Those dark eyes came back and stuck with me for what seemed like generations, ones that stretched from a fire in a Catholic church in Naperville to a rundown farmhouse in Indiana. Then she shook her head. "Maybe later. And he didn't kill anybody. I don't believe that."

"Then help me figure out who did."

"I'll give you a ride to Crown Lake. It's the next town."

A light bulb clicked on somewhere in a sleep-deprived brain. "Make it Morristown, and you've got a deal."

"A deal for what?"

"Whatever you want. Just make it Morristown."

Her eyes searched the ceiling again. "Okay, let's go. It'll take a good half hour. He should sleep a lot longer than that."

She strolled outside and aimed for the Explorer. On the way to the car I noticed the full stalks of corn in well-tended fields that appeared out of place set against the run-down farm buildings. "Let me guess. You guys own the house and live in it, but you lease the fields?"

"Good guess. What were your clues?"

"Well, from the looks of this place and the work habits of you three, I couldn't see you all actually doing this." I pointed to the fields. "So what gives? Why aren't you farming anymore?"

Ms. Big Eyes stood in the open door of her car, regarding me with light amusement. "If you understood that, you'd realize what this is all about."

She never bothered to explain, though. In fact, she didn't say another word all the way to Morristown. I gave her my card and asked her to call if anything came up. I caught her looking over at me several times, even staring once. But she never said anything.

It was a bit after 9:00 when we got there. I asked Sheila to drop me off at the Starbuck's across from the courthouse, where I picked up a cup of overpriced but drinkable coffee. I also grabbed a muffin. Once I felt relatively safe, at least beyond the clutches of my new friends from Indiana, I realized how hungry I was. Then I waited.

About 40 minutes later I saw Alison Peterson stroll by on her way to work. I ran out of the store and waited until I was about five feet behind her before calling out.

"Well, hello, Alison. Fancy meeting you here." It was a little early for me to be all that creative.

She must have recognized my voice, because she spun around with a look of sheer amazement on her face. "You! Aren't you that fellow from Illinois? What are you doing here?"

I nodded and walked closer. "That's right. Can I buy you a cup of coffee?"

"But I'm on my way to work." She seemed suddenly to see the rest of me, the morning hairdo that stuck out in clumps at odd angles, the wrinkled shirt and pants, the pale skin, the scraggily beard. Her expression changed from one of surprise to one of concern, maybe even a bit of disgust when she found the clot of blood at the back of my skull. "What happened? Are you all right?"

"Well, I was kidnapped." I probed the back of head with very careful fingers. "I'll be okay, but I could use your help."

"Why don't you go to the police?"

"I will eventually. But right now I think you're the only person I can trust."

"Don't be ridiculous. You hardly know me." Now her face had a maternal look of concern.

"Perhaps that's why. Please, I can explain inside." I gestured toward the Starbucks. "Don't worry, we won't be alone."

"Well, perhaps I have enough time for just one cup."

We walked indoors, where I bought another coffee and a muffin. Then we found our former table by the window.

"You seem to prefer this spot."

I shrugged. "It lets me keep an eye on who's outside."

"Are you really that worried?"

"I am now. That's why I need you help."

I explained part of what had occurred during the night, the part where I had gone to the Burkhardt house on Edgewater and been waylaid by the Big Fella, who I assumed was associated with the Harbours. I left out the part about the body. I told her how I had come to find myself in Morristown, Indiana on a sunny June morning and how I was now stranded miles from home and miles from my car.

"So what do you want me to do?"

"Well, a lift home would really help."

"And what about my job?"

"Can't you call in sick?"

"Perhaps. But I still don't understand why you can't go

to the police. They'll give you a ride, won't they?"

"Maybe, and maybe not. You see, I can't really go to the police here, since the folks at that farm will just deny everything. I don't have any proof. The whole story sounds wildly implausible. I mean, you probably have doubts about my sanity right now as well." Her eyebrows arched. "So you see, I really am stuck."

Her hands played with the buttons on the collar of her blue cotton blouse, and her gaze drifted from the coffee to my face. "I guess you are in trouble. But..." She bit her lip, "I hardly know you."

"You're right. And I appreciate your concern. But I'm asking you to trust me. Is there anything I can do to convince you that I'm on the level?"

She thought for a moment. "Not really. Not in this situation. But I guess I'll try." She glanced through the window at the courthouse. "Let me go give them some kind of excuse, and we can meet at my car. It's a green Honda Civic over in the city lot. Space Q63."

"Thanks so much. I'll meet you there."

I waited for her to disappear inside the courthouse building before I jumped from the booth and headed for her car. 15 minutes later, Alison walked up to the driver's side. Unfortunately, she wasn't alone. A local patrolman in a uniform of gray and blue, a set of Foster Grants, and an artificial smile marched by her side.

I held up my hands. "I guess I should have known better." I sighed. "I can't say as I really blame you."

The cop spoke while Alison bit her lip and looked off at some speck in the distance. "Would you come with me, sir?"

I really didn't have any choice. I shrugged, nodded, then waved to Alison Peterson as we walked past her on our way to the station.

Morristown had one of those police stations you expect to find in a small Midwestern town. Tailored to local history and experience, of course. I almost expected to find an altar in this one, given the town reputation for promoting matrimony way back when. This one sat, sans altar, in the block behind the courthouse, so we didn't have far to walk. It was also built in the same American gothic style and probably with materials from the same limestone pit. A couple black and white cruisers caught their breath out front, and another sailed into the parking lot when we arrived. My host and the driver exchanged smiles, probably like they do whenever they deliver some looney to the drunk tank. Lord knows it was about how I felt at this point.

We strolled past the front desk, where the duty sergeant looked up from his logbook, tossing the same smile at my companion. We ended up in an office at the back occupied by an older, heavy-set man, somewhere in his late fifties or early sixties I guessed, based on the closely cropped gray hair and budding stomach. He also looked like the chief. It was my detective training again. I noticed the name plate on his desk: Chief Albert Peterson. Oh shit, I thought.

"Don't tell me Alison's your daughter?"

He leaned back in his swivel chair and tucked a fist under his chin. Sunlight from the two windows framed his desk in twin sets of shadowed rectangles and sparkled momentarily off his reading glasses. The room also smelled of old smoke despite the "no smoking" sign posted over the door. The patrolman grabbed a corner of the desk with his butt.

"Niece. And she had quite a tale to tell. You got any identification?"

Fortunately, that was one thing I still did possess, having lost my dignity some time earlier that morning. I pulled out my wallet and tossed my driver's license and a copy of my PI's license on the desk. Chief Peterson picked both up and studied them like some ancient manuscript. I couldn't be sure, but I think I saw his lips moving. But then, he may have only been talking to himself. I do that occasionally as well. The patrolman leaned over to get a good view himself, until the chief shot him a look that not only straightened his back but knocked him off the desk, too. His name tag read Franklin.

"Okay, this looks legit. Now, why don't you tell me what happened, in your words. Alison sounded a bit confused."

So I did. I gave him most of it, anyway, leaving out the parts about the notebooks, the fire, and all that interesting historical stuff. I told him how a client had been killed and that when I was checking his house after the police were through, I had been jumped and keelhauled across the state line.

"So they brought you over here with a ship?" Franklin asked.

"You know what I mean." I wanted to add "asshole," but I figured I was in enough trouble as it was.

"Well, however they did it, it's still a federal offense," the chief said.

"But we don't want to bring those guys in just yet, do we?" I almost winked.

"Why," the chief pressed, "you wanna go back there to that farmhouse and kick some ass?"

"At some point, sure. But there's another issue here."

"And that would be?"

"Another murder." I gave him the details, as best I knew them, of course, on the demise of Charlie Harbour, and how it might be linked to the earlier death of Ray Burkhardt.

"You reported this yet?"

I spread my hands wide. "I really haven't had the chance yet, have I?"

A meaty hand at the end of a muscled, hairy forearm extending from a rolled-up sleeve pushed the telephone in my direction. "You do now."

So I called the Naperville PD. Luckily Jamieson was in. I got another one of those "sheeet" outbursts when I told him what I had found at the Edgewater address.

"What are you gonna tell Hardy, Rick?"

"I'll think of something. Pass me over to the chief, would you?"

Chief Peterson took the receiver with that departmental stare of emotional neutrality, while the patrolman looked at me like I had just arrived from Mars. He had also reclaimed his seat on the corner of the chief's desk. Peterson did some nodding, grunted once or twice, and then spoke several complete sentences.

"No, no. That's all right. I'll bring him back. I'd kind of like to identify the body. I've had a few run-ins with Charlie Harbour myself." There was a pause. "No, he wasn't a model citizen, and no, I won't miss him." Another pause. "My pleasure. We've gotten to know your friend real well in this town. We'll see you in about two hours."

He dunked the receiver in its cradle, then took in the patrolman with a look that swept him off the desk again. "Get me the keys to a cruiser with a full tank of gas." Then he looked at me. "We're goin' for a ride. It's time to go home and identify a corpse."

Outside, none other than Alison Peterson was standing by one of the patrol cars. Or rather, she was pacing back and forth at the trunk. When she saw us she stopped, wheeled with her hands folded in front of her, a broad smile pasted on her face. I was actually relieved that someone in this town knew how to smile, even if it wasn't real. It sure made me feel a lot more appreciated, though, than those nods from the cops.

"Where are we going, Uncle Al?"

"Takin' him home." He rolled his head in my direction. "Why?"

"Naperville? Then I'm going, too."

"What the hell for?"

"Because I feel badly about all this." She stepped toward us, her eyes bright and sparkling with some kind of late spring joy and enthusiasm. She was also biting her lip again, which I was beginning to recognize as her main move when she was uncertain or wanted something. But it was also endearing the way she did it. "Mr. Habermann came to me for help, and I just turned him over to you and your henchmen."

I figured I'd better intervene at this point, since I really couldn't complain about my treatment. "Oh, they were very hospitable, Alison." I turned toward the chief. "A donut would've been nice, though."

"Shaddup, you." I guessed he didn't like to share. "Look, Alison. This is official police business, and I am not bringing a civilian along, no matter how closely related we are."

She pivoted in the direction of her Civic, which I noticed just then was parked next to one of the cruisers. "Then I'm going to follow you in my own car. I took the day off. I was really too upset with myself to work."

She wheeled once more and started toward her car. I glanced around at some cops milling around at the station entrance, eager to catch the show. The fact that they all wore huge smiles, much more sincere than the ones they had given me, suggested that this was not the first encounter between the chief and his niece at the station, and that this one would probably turn out like all the others.

"Goddammit!" The chief looked at me like it was my fault, which it was, kind of. "Get in the goddamn car, Alison." He looked back at the entrance, which had suddenly grown empty, and shouted so that those waiting just inside the door could hear. "If I ever hear about any of this from anyone, Charlie Harbour will not be the only new corpse around."

That brought several pairs of eyes, mostly blue and hazel, around the corner of the door frame. I think I heard a "No shit?" or two. A "Charlie Harbour?" as well.

I offered Alison the chance to ride shotgun, but she opted for the back seat, "where Uncle Al always makes me sit."

"She's not even supposed to be here, dammit," he grumbled.

Then we all piled into a brand new police cruiser with a full tank of gas like one big happy family.

CHAPTER NINE

We took the ugly route. I didn't see a whole lot of it, though, because I was either sleeping or listening to Chief Peterson. He decided to fill me in on the personal history of Charlie Harbour while we drove to Naperville to identify the body. I had asked if we could drive past the farmhouse where I had recently been a guest.

"That'll wait," he said. "Those folks aren't goin' nowhere." His deep blue eyes, pooled in layers of flesh, considered my face. "First things first, Habermann. We got a dead man to see. And if he is who you say he is, it'll be real interesting."

"Why's that?"

"Because that farmhouse you described sounds a lot like the Harbour place."

Alison sat in the back seat on the passenger side, right behind me. Chief Peterson tossed a glance and a scowl at the back seat as we wound our way through town toward Route 65. "Ever since she broke up with that half-assed moron she married, I can't say no to her."

"What makes him half-assed?"

"Oh, hell, the jerk refused to start a family. Said he had his career to consider...."

"What did he do?"

"Marketing Rep,' he calls it. I say 'salesman.'" He saw my eyebrows rise. "Hospital equipment. Anyway, the son-of-a-bitch moved in with a waitress, and now he's got two kids."

"He forgot to have his girlfriend practice safe sex," Alison explained.

I pivoted toward her voice. I had expected some sign of distress or depression, like maybe tears or even a frown. Instead, she wore the same smile she had used on us back at the station, as though everything had turned out just right.

"He was kind of an asshole," she added.

Chief Peterson snorted. "Yeah, well, whatever." The car stormed up the entrance ramp and onto Route 65, barreling north toward Gary. Sun washed the blacktop, turning it a bright gray. A semi hauling a load of fuel bundled past in the left lane, and a brown Mercedes roared up on our rear. It backed off quickly, though, as soon as its driver recognized the rack of lights across the top of our car. I thought I could get used to riding in one of these.

"So, whatcha know about the Harbour character?" the chief asked.

"Next to nothin'." I relayed what little I had gleaned from the Nexus articles, and the chief chuckled at that.

"Shit, son, Charlie Harbour was a real case. I only nailed him for a B & E and a DUI, but other cops in the area got him for that and a lot more. Mostly got reduced to misdemeanor stuff, unfortunately. You know, stuff that put him in the county jail for a short stay."

"So he never did any hard time?"

"I wouldn't say that. He did a couple years for aggravated assault. That boy had a real temper. He also got grabbed once for attempted arson, but it was reduced to another B & E when he copped a plea."

"Not one of your model Hoosiers, eh"

Peterson shook his head. "Nope. They'll probably be quite a few brewskies hoisted this evening by many of my colleagues to toast the passing of that particular toad."

"So, what do you think happened? Did he overreach, run into something too big for him to handle?"

The chief shrugged. "Can't really say until I know more. But I wouldn't be surprised. Maybe one of his old white power chums decided to take him out." His head rotated slowly in my direction, as though waiting for me to respond. "Or some competition."

"Competition for what?" I stared out the windshield for a bit. "So, was he connected to the Klan or whatever they call themselves these days?" Only then did I look over at the chief.

He shrugged. "It's hard to tell what they call themselves from day to day. But yeah, he had some ties there." He returned my gaze. "I never could tell if he really believed it or just liked the trouble-makin' possibilites."

"Well, I guess I won't get the chance to ask him now."

His gaze returned to the interstate. "I wouldn't want to run into whoever it was that put him down, though, not in a dark alley or the middle of the street. Charlie Harbour was one tough customer."

I noticed then that his eyes were aimed at the rearview mirror as he said this, studying the reaction of his niece. I snuck a peek at the back seat myself, but Alison's eyes, and probably her attention, had moved on, mapping the many vacuous billboards that bordered the soulless landscape outside the window.

Alison shook me awake. At least, I was pretty sure the small hand and thin fingers belonged to her, since they did not remind me of the paw that had passed me the telephone back in Morristown. She also left her hand on my shoulder just a moment longer after I had stirred, and I appreciated those soft, tan fingers. The ring finger had a thin white line, suggesting that she had only recently removed her wedding band. I thought for a moment whether anything I had heard would indicate if she was a recent divorcee, or whether she was the type to hold on to a ring in the hope that the marriage could be saved. Not that it mattered, not to me anyway. Besides, it hurt to think too much just then. It was about all I could manage just to give Peterson directions to the Burkhardt house.

I must have nodded off again, because the next thing I

knew Chief Peterson was already stepping out of the car and moving toward the house. Only then did I realize we were at the Burkhardt place on Edgewater. A crowd had gathered across the street, collecting in small clots under the trees to whisper their worries and assumptions to each other. A thick strip of evidence tape cut the yard and driveway off from the rest of the world, and Jamieson's Thunderbird sat at the curb, framed by a couple of patrol cars. We had dropped the Indiana cruiser at the curb across the street, which set off a new buzz among the onlookers. A housewife pointed at me, and I heard her ask her neighbor if she thought I was the killer. Given my look, I really couldn't blame her. Still, I was a bit pissed. We locals needed to stick together. Alison smiled and let go a small laugh.

A familiar-looking cop, Ziegler, according to his name tag, nodded and let us pass at the edge of the driveway. Our paths had crossed before, and when he saw me sandwiched between Peterson and his niece, Ziegler just shook his head and frowned. I marked him as someone who'd never go far unless he developed some imagination. That, at least, made me a feel a little better.

We marched to the backyard and patio, and then through the kitchen door. Jamieson's back stared at us from the living room, while the techies scurried around getting photographs, bagging stuff, and checking for prints. The county coroner passed by on his way out but slowed to take us in when he reached the kitchen. I had never realized that a dark blue suit could get so wrinkled. Maybe if he had been wearing a tie he wouldn't have looked so scruffy. Some hair on the top of his head would have helped, too. He was pulling his plastic gloves off when he recognized me, and that brought him to a complete halt.

"Sometimes, Habermann, I wonder what you do to find all this trouble."

"You act like it was all my fault, Doc."

"Well, you're the reason he was here, aren't you?"

"Not exactly. And while we're at it, maybe you should leave the detective work to the pros, Doc, and go fix another nose or somethin'."

That got me another head-shake, something like the one from Ziegler. I think I preferred the wry smiles back in Morristown. "You're lucky you've got friends like Rick there." He nodded in Jamieson's direction. "Though I'm not sure why."

"He sees qualities in me you can only guess at, you quack. Now go study for your gynecology exams. I think I saw a *Hustler* in your car outside." He started for the door. "And you can bet I'll be going elsewhere for my flu shot this year."

That got me my third head-shake. He also flipped me the bird.

"Kind of hard on him, weren't you?" Peterson asked.

"Oh, he'll get over it," I replied. "Besides, I feel like shit, and he seemed as good a target as anyone."

"Have you two known each other long?" Alison asked.

"Yeah, we went to Saints Peter and Paul together. He's still pissed that I never picked him for any of my softball teams. Besides, I punched him once when he wouldn't lend me a dollar."

We walked into the living room, where Jamieson turned, introduced himself, and shook hands all around. He was attired a lot more professionally this time with gray cotton slacks, a white dress shirt and blue blazer. He also smelled like Old Spice when you got close enough to escape the stench of death building up in the room and passing through the house. He pointed at the techies and looked at me. "I suppose most of those prints they find will be yours."

"Well, some for sure," I replied.

"And this?" He held out a baggie with the dish towel.

"Yeah," I conceded. "That's my blood." I explained

how it got there.

"Tell me more. The whole thing, in fact."

I did, reminding him that a local law enforcement official had suggested I stop by.

"Not quite, Bill," Jamieson said.

"Well, maybe not explicitly or in so many words. But you sure as hell let me know nothing would be here to stop me. By the way," I glanced around, "where's the boss?" I realized only then that I hadn't seen Hardy's Chrysler outside.

"He was here but had to split." I raised my eyebrows. "He had to get back for a budget meeting. He'll want to see you, though."

"No doubt. What should I tell him?"

"The truth." Jamieson cracked a smile that barely broke the corners of his mouth. "Or most of it."

Our comradely exchange was interrupted by Chief Peterson. He had moved over to the corpse, lifted the sheet off the face, and was squatting next to it. He let the sheet fall back in place, stood up, and pulled a pair of gloves off his hands. He must have brought his own, because I never saw him borrow a pair from anyone else.

"I hate to complicate matters here, boys, but...."

"What is it, Chief?" I asked.

"It seems you got more mysteries than you realize. So do I, for that matter."

"How so?" Jamieson pressed.

"This," he gestured toward the body, "is not Charlie Harbour."

That "sheeet" sound erupted from Jamieson again.

"Oh, my God!" Alison yelled.

"What the hell is going on?" I asked. Actually, I nearly shouted. I stumbled toward the corpse, as if that might change something. "Just who the fuck is it?"

"Easy, son." Peterson nodded in Alison's direction.

"There's a lady present."

"Sorry." I liked his way of reminding me a lot better than Sheila's ear twist.

"I'm not really sure," he added, looking at Jamieson. "Your boys didn't find a wallet or any kind of identification, did they?" Jamieson shook his head. "If you give me a set of prints, then I'll run them through our records or send 'em on down to Indianapolis to see if that helps."

"Should we go to Washington?" Jamieson asked.

"Oh, let's not just yet. Let's you and I see what we can figure out here first." Jamieson smiled first, and then Peterson followed. "We'll have to bring in the feds eventually, of course," Peterson continued, "since we got an inter-state case here. But there's no need to rush. That's how mistakes get made."

Jamieson held out his hand. "Chief, I like the way you work. And I think this could be the beginning of a long friendship."

Alison's smile had also returned. She grabbed my forearm and gave it a squeeze. I wasn't sure what to make of that.

Alison had to wake me again when we reached my place. I threw a forearm over my eyes as sunlight burned through the windshield. Then I peeled my shirt from my back, where the sweat had glued them together. "Wake me when we get there."

"We are there, son." Chief Peterson blew out some breath, probably in frustration.

I pushed myself up against the back of the front seat, squinting at all the blue, cloudless sky. I remembered that one was supposed to welcome this kind of weather, but I just wanted a longer, deeper night to help me catch up on the sleep I felt I had earned. "Geez, I'm sorry. Come on up and let me fix you both some coffee. If my food is still good, I'll even make you some breakfast."

I heard the driver's door open and glanced over in time to see the chief climb from the car and wave. I turned and found Jamieson pulling in behind us.

"You bet you will," Alison said. "But you'll have to make us lunch. We've already had breakfast. So have you, back at Starbucks."

"Good point." Actually, I couldn't remember that far back just then, but I was not inclined to argue.

We scrambled across the street and up the back stairs. I was actually looking forward to playing host for my new friends. That is, until I found Chief Hardy standing at my sink, smoking a cigarette, and flicking the ashes on my floor.

"Did you knock at least? And since when did you start smoking?"

"I knocked, but nobody answered," Hardy replied. He studied the stick between his fingers. "And this comes from havin' you around so much, Habermann. You're bad for my health." Smoke curled around his white shirt, maroon tie, and brown plaid jacket. I wasn't helping his fashion sense either, apparently.

"Very funny. Where's your car?" My question reminded me that we had left my own over by the Burkhardt place.

"In the alley. Where's yours?"

"How convenient. And you know where mine is, so let's not get cute."

"Cute?"

"That's right. I'm also going to have to get my key back from Jamieson. There's this thing called privacy." I turned to Chief Peterson and Alison, who had followed me in along with Jamieson. "Chief, meet the chief. You guys should have a lot to talk about. You know, trade war stories, stuff like that."

They shook hands. Jamieson joined us, then everyone

stood around in awkward silence. Hardy ran tap water over his smoke, then left it in the sink.

"Thanks for not littering. Does your wife let you live like that?"

He shrugged and gave me one of his blank stares. "She's not here."

"Let's all grab a seat at the table," I suggested. "Maybe we can trade information, or brainstorm, or something. If not, then I'll grab a shower. It's been a long 36 hours."

"We'll be quick, Bill." Jamieson had dropped into a seat next to mine. Alison sat to my left, her uncle next to her. Hardy placed himself right across from me with a grunt and a grumble.

Alison stood up, walked as far as the entrance to my living room, then stopped as though she had hit a wall. Her eyes went wide and her mouth wrinkled. She had just encountered my trashed apartment.

"Oh my God, Bill. Do you live like this?"

"Only when someone has broken in and rummaged through my place."

Peterson stood up as well, glanced over her shoulder, then sat back down. "Our friends?"

I nodded. "That's my guess."

"Yes, Alison," Hardy added, "he really does live like that." He turned to me. "You got any coffee?"

"You could've made some while you waited, Frank."

"I was too busy looking for your dirty magazines."

"Mine have too many words for you, Frank."

"Gentlemen," Alison scolded, "let's get down to business. I'll make the coffee if you'll discuss the case. I need to get back to Morristown sometime today."

She jumped up and walked over to the sink, where she filled the pot with water, poured it into the machine, then proceeded to slam all my cupboard doors looking for the coffee.

"He keeps it in the freezer," Jamieson said. "I'm not sure why."

"Thank you, Rick," she replied. Her index finger rolled in the air. "The rest of you get to work."

Peterson spoke to Hardy. "As I told the others here, the body you have does not belong to Charlie Harbour. I think it's a small-time hood from the fringe of the white power scene, but I'm not sure."

"And you said Charlie Harbour had ties to these groups, or group."

Peterson flopped his hand back and forth. "Sort of. As I said, I think he just liked to stir up trouble. He wasn't the kind to make speeches."

"You think there might be something to this Klan business?" Hardy asked.

"Oh, hell, I don't know about that," Peterson replied with a frown. "Those guys have been pretty fragmented and insignificant for years now. And I haven't seen Harbour mixed up in that kind of activity for a while."

"But still, they could always revive," Jamieson suggested.

"Yeah, perhaps," Peterson conceded. "But a lot's changed. That doesn't mean there couldn't be some of them after that money you mentioned."

"How would they know about it?" Jamieson pressed.

The chief frowned and studied his hands. "That's a good question. I doubt that sort of information is available to a whole lot of people. It's something I'll have to explore.'"

"Still, you think this Charlie Harbour could be behind these killings?" Hardy asked. "Could he have assembled a group of neo-nazis to find this stash?"

"Maybe," Peterson nodded, looking up. "The question is, why assemble a group?"

"How long has this search been going on?" Jamieson added. "If there is one."

"Just a minute,," I interrupted. "We aren't even sure there is any money. And this whole thing appears to have started long ago. We haven't established any link between the two series of events yet."

"But it would explain why Harbour and others would be roaming around here in Illinois," Peterson noted. "Is there anything else that links them to your other killing? Have you all gotten very far on that one?"

Jamieson glanced at the table and shook his head. Then he quickly looked up. "What do you know about the Harbours?"

"I already gave your friend here a rundown on the kind of jerk Charlie is," Peterson replied.

"How about the rest of the family?" I pressed.

"I don't really know much. There's just Charlie and his sister Sheila left, as far as I know. You sure there was another woman at that place?"

I nodded. "Yeah, blonde and heavy. She seemed to be attached to my host."

"Sounds like Charlie's common-law wife," Peterson continued. "A woman named Mary Wilson. My guess is that you had a run-in with 'ol Charlie himself."

"Wonderful. Was that their farm?"

"I think so. As I said, that sounds like the place you mentioned. The family had some land south of town but lost a big chunk of it before the war."

"How and when?" Jamieson continued.

Peterson shrugged. "Not really sure. You know, Alison?" Peterson half-turned in his chair to catch his niece, who stood by the sink, coffee dripping into the pot at her side.

"I don't recall either. Never really heard much about it, since they weren't from Morristown." Her smile faded. She stared long and hard at her uncle, and her lips seemed to go hard and tight, almost brittle.

"I thought one of the Harbours was mayor back in the

20s," I said.

"If that's what you say," Peterson replied. "But that was probably about it. If he was connected to the KKK, he probably quit that sort of thing when the Klan's power broke in the State. But we can always check it out. Why? You think this Klan thing is really so important?"

"Could be," I replied. "I mean, we haven't got a whole lot else to go on. And Charlie—if that's who it was—said there was something else besides the money. It sounded as though that was almost incidental, though. And right now I'd say that anything that carries us closer to the fire that destroyed our church and the shooting of Carl Harbour in 1922 will bring us closer to solving this puzzle. I'm pretty sure it's why two people are dead already."

I turned to Peterson. "Why do you think Charlie Harbour lied about the identity of the dead man?"

Chief Peterson shrugged. "Why not? He's a jerk-off, and he probably enjoyed pulling your chain." He opened, then closed his hands with a shrug, glancing at Alison. "And he is a bad one all right. I don't doubt he's capable of killing someone in a rage."

"But will, or can, he keep killing?" Hardy asked.

"I guess that depends on just what he's after, and how valuable this prize is. If that's what's really behind it." He seemed to ponder the thought for a moment. "Yeah, I'd say it could happen again."

"You think there'll be more murders?" Hardy asked. He turned to me. "They do seem to have a habit of turning up on your watch, Habermann."

"Well, Frank, I guess that means we'll have to solve this case real quick."

"Why don't you folks do what you've got to do here over at the Burkhardt house," Peterson suggested, "and let me run down a few things on my end? I'll take care of the Indiana side of this business, and we'll see if this all really is connected."

Heads nodded in unison all around the table.

"So that's the church," Alison announced after a moment's silence. She strolled over to the window behind the kitchen table.

"Well, that's the church that was built on the ashes of the one that burned down in 1922," I corrected her.

"Can we go inside?" she wondered aloud, as she pivoted toward us. We had all followed her gaze out the window, as though seeing the church for the first time. "Let's do, Uncle Al. I'd like to see what the fuss is all about." Her smile was back. "Then we can drive back. We'll take some coffee with us. That's okay, isn't it?"

I assured her it was. In fact, we all poured a cup, then wandered down the stairs and across the street. Jamieson and Hardy peeled off to their cars to return to the station. I walked with Alison and her Uncle Al to the church, which was empty this early in the afternoon. Recess at Peter and Paul was also over, so we had the grounds pretty much to ourselves.

Alison sauntered up and down the aisles, marveling at the stained glass windows and the graphic art in the Stations of the Cross. The chief and I waited in the back, just inside the middle doors. For a brief moment I considered telling Chief Peterson the story of how much trouble I got into in seventh grade during a Lenten service when we'd go through the Stations at morning Mass. I let it pass when I saw how uncomfortable he was. "Let me guess, you're a Protestant."

He chuckled. "You got it. You an altar boy?"

"Not anymore."

That got some more laughter.

"Let me ask you something, Chief."

"Shoot."

"I noticed in the car and in my kitchen that you tried to

include Alison in the conversation a couple times, or at least seemed to be gauging her reaction. Was I imagining that?"

Peterson, who had kept his eyes on his niece the whole time we were in the church, turned toward me. Colored light streamed through one of the windows and seemed to wrap him in a rainbow-like halo. "No, you didn't imagine that." He paused long enough to weigh the character of his younger relative as she made her way toward the door. "Her husband had gotten himself stuck in some of Charlie Harbour's troubles. Charlie was bad enough, but hubby also had a mean streak that really scared her."

"So it wasn't just about starting a family?"

Peterson shrugged again. "Well, Alison did want to have kids, but she knew it wasn't going to happen with that creep."

"But he's out of it now?"

"Says he is." Peterson turned to go, waving at Alison. "But I plan to check on it when I get back. It's as good a place as any to start." The colored light behind his head burst across the center aisle, and I realized he had been standing in a direct line from the sun to the window. When she reached us, Alison passed through the bright, multi-hued rays like she was transparent.

"Odd, though," I said to Peterson.

"What's that?"

"That Alison knew so much about the church fire. She recognized the story as soon as I mentioned it."

Peterson frowned, his gaze never leaving Alison. "Yeah, that is odd. I'll have to ask her about it."

I asked the Hoosiers to drop me at my car back near Edgewater on their way to the interstate so I could drive it home. I had almost forgotten again that I had left it there. Lack of sleep will do that to you. When I got to Gartner Street I saw that some prick had given me a parking ticket.

I spent the afternoon running errands around town—mostly getting some fresh food and drinks for my place—and trying to finish putting my apartment back together. The most important errand, though, was at Nichols Library, where I remembered that a list from the Indiana Historical Society might be waiting for me. And it was.

"This arrived two days ago," the librarian said. She was wearing a denim sack that passed for a skirt and something that looked like burlap for a blouse. "I was beginning to think you had forgotten."

"No, no chance of that. Some other work came up that I had to address first." I held the papers aloft, almost like a trophy, I was so glad. "But thanks very much. May I keep this?"

Her face registered a confused look similar to the expression she wore the first time we spoke. Her left hand rose to her face and stroked her lips and chin, while her eyes narrowed, as though I was hard to see. She did not respond.

"I'll just take this with me then, if you don't mind." I backed toward the entrance. "You've been very helpful. I promise to pay my property taxes. Thanks again."

Once outside I trotted to the Cabrio and studied the list. There were a lot of pages. The KKK had clearly been a popular organization in Indiana during the 1920s, and I had to scan through every page several times to be certain. But there was no Carl Harbour listed. And no Randolph Harbour either. In fact, there were no Harbours at all.

I tossed the pile on the front seat and called Jamieson to tell him I was returning to Indiana to pay a call on the farmhouse. I informed him that I was actually on my way, even as we spoke.

"Have you left town yet?" he asked.

"You mean Naperville?"

"That's right, Shamus. You know many others that

would apply?"

"Sorry, but it's been a long night," I apologized. "And no, I'm not out of town yet. I'm just crossing Washington. Why?"

"Because I'm coming with you."

"What the hell for?"

"Because, Billy-boy, you need me. And no more arguments. I'll meet you at your place in 30 minutes."

I was too tired to argue. So I figured maybe it was a good thing Jamieson was coming along after all.

CHAPTER TEN

"Okay, Rick, you want to tell me why you insisted on coming along? And while you're at it, you can tell why me you guys don't want to call in the feds."

"What about you? Why are you so hot to run back into Indiana?"

"I asked you first."

At that point we were crossing the state line into the home of the Hoosiers. We were riding in his car, since Jamieson claimed I had too many bags under my eyes to drive myself. With a map and a memory only partly fogged from lack of sleep and creeping middle age, I had been able to retrace my journey from the night before. We only lost the path once, when I took us all the way south to Kankakee. But after we found Route 41 inside Indiana, I knew we were on the right track.

"I can't speak for Peterson, but I'm not prepared to give this case to those pricks from Hooverville," Rick claimed. "Not yet."

"Why not?"

"Because they would love to get their hands on this thing. And you and I would be out of it, Bill. This is our case."

"Our case? You haven't seemed all that convinced so far. When did you convert?"

"I'm not sure I'd go that far. But I just don't see any competition out there right now. The killing at the Burkhardt place and the involvement of this Charlie Harbour make for some convincing links."

"And Hardy's okay with this?"

He shrugged. "Not really. Actually, he's not aware of it."

"That's reassuring." I considered this unwelcome news for a moment but figured it was too late to do anything about it now. "So, how we gonna play it?"

"Why are you askin' me? This is your trip." He smiled and shook his head again.. "Besides, you're the one who's been here before." Jamieson's brow furrowed, as though he had just discovered something unpleasant. "Tell me why we're here again, and so soon?"

I studied the fields to our right. The sun sprayed the land that stretched out against the horizon with a glare that seemed to turn the color dial a shade lower. The rich farmland with its dark soil had actually been dimmed by the brightness of the sun, if that was possible. I peered through the cornstalks and trees and asked myself that same question: Why I was chasing the pipe dream of a dead man? Maybe it was because he was just that, dead. And he'd had a dream I had dismissed. I thought about it for a minute more, but I couldn't be sure. I knew I wanted to find out before I went home, though.

"Something about this case has pissed me off," I said.

"Well, no shit."

"No, it's not just that I was jumped and dragged over here. Sure, that brought me in deeper than before. But I'm not about to leave everything to the locals and simply walk away. Not by a long shot, goddammit." Jamieson gave me one of those wide-eyed looks of wonder. "I mean it," I continued. Besides, it was our church that burned down and started this whole thing. At least, it seems like it."

"And the KKK angle?"

"Things aren't exactly falling into place there," I admitted.

We rode in silence for another mile. "Okay, you're the professional," I said. How do you want to handle this thing?"

Jamieson glanced over at me and shook his head. "Give me a fucking break. Like you've ever needed or wanted guidance from 'the professionals,' as you call us. Besides, you were once one of us yourself."

I thought for a moment, but I couldn't come up with a plan. I was too tired to lie. "We'll have to ad hoc it."

"Say what?"

I gave him one of those looks suggesting he had so much to learn, like fathers get from their teenaged children that tells them how much they've aged. "We'll have to play it by ear. I haven't really thought that far ahead," I confessed.

"Now that's what I call reassuring." Jamieson smiled and shook his head.

I studied my friend. His attention was focused on the road, which was a good thing since I was in no shape to drive. This must have been one big adventure for him. Gunslinger Private Eye Sam Spade Jamieson. He was ready for action, dressed in a black T-shirt and black jeans, like he expected to blend with the night. We'd be lucky to get back to Illinois alive if we ran into trouble, if only because my own outfit of blue jeans and a faded green polo would probably make for a great target. I was not that into camouflage. Not since Vietnam.

They still hadn't painted the place by the time we arrived. The LeSabre was also gone, but the Explorer was parked in its usual spot by the back porch. If we had planned on a stealth approach, the element of surprise had probably been lost when the tires crunched over the gravel in the driveway. That guess was confirmed when the screen door creaked open and Sheila walked onto the back stoop. She had on the same jeans and sneakers from this morning, but in place of the long-sleeved gray T-shirt, she had on a very feminine short-sleeved, yellow blouse that showcased her upper figure a lot better than the T-shirt. The ladylike appearance did not go with the Glock 9mm semi-automatic she was carrying, however. Jamieson probably figured at this point that he was the smart one, that maybe she wouldn't see him in his black camouflage, even though it was only dusk. Whatever the time, though, I was pretty sure I made a good target.

I stepped out of the car, and Jamieson did likewise. I didn't move toward the house, though. Not yet.

"Where are the others, Sheila?" I called out.

"Who wants to know?"

"Well, I do." I started slowly toward the stoop. "That's why I asked."

"You really are a smart ass, even if you are good lookin'. In an ugly sort of way."

I tried my disarming smile, part of the ad hoc approach. "Why, Sheila, I wasn't sure you had noticed. I was hoping you had, because I sure noticed you." That was true, too. But mostly I said it because I hoped it would keep that Glock pointed away from me and at the ground.

The semi-automatic moved easily up and down the side of her leg. I remembered then the speed and ease with which she had caught me in the chair that very morning. And I did not think it was entirely because I had been so tired.

"You can come up, but keep a few feet between us," she said.

"You seem awfully suspicious, Sheila," Jamieson said. "What are you afraid of?"

"And who might you be?" Those raven-hued eyes bored in on Jamieson.

"I'm the law."

Just what I had not wanted him to say.

Sheila just laughed. "They've already been here, thanks to you." The eyes and pistol swung toward me again. "I suppose the first thing you did was run to the police, you pussy."

"Now Sheila, someone called the police on me when I wandered into Morristown. I had to tell them something."

"Then why'd you want to go there in the first place? I thought you had friends there."

"Well, I thought I did, too. I guess I was wrong."

The Glock pointed at the Thunderbird. "That your

car?"

"No," I explained. "It belongs to my friend here. The style's a little out of date for me. I also don't care for the mileage."

She rolled her eyes and turned to Jamieson. "Then if you are the law, I'll bet you're from Naperville, judgin' by that Illinois plate." She looked back at me. "See, I can play detective, too." Suddenly, her eyes widened, then narrowed, and a pair of deep dark ice picks were aimed at me. The Glock waved at me again, too. "You said you didn't trust them."

"He's a friend, Sheila. He may be a cop, but I've known him since I was a kid. We grew up together. And we're trying to figure this thing out together."

"So, what have you got now?"

"I think that this house and farm belong to your family, and that you're all that's left of the Harbours. I want to know how you came to this place and this time. And how it is that you're mixed up in whatever it is your brother Charlie's after."

"How'd you figure all that? How'd you get his name? And what about those other dead people?"

"Still dead, Sheila. And I think Charlie knows why, if he didn't kill them himself."

That's when I found the bruise on her arm. I pointed to it. "Is that why you wore a long-sleeve shirt earlier today?"

She shrugged. "I didn't have it then. Charlie was pretty pissed when he found out you were gone. Said he wanted to talk to you some more. That's why I got this." She hefted the pistol.

"For protection? Against Charlie?"

"No, butthead. To make sure you assholes clear off. I want you gone before Charlie gets back"

"Why don't you want us here when Charlie returns?" Jamieson asked.

"Because I'm tryin' to avoid more trouble."

I closed the gap between us and stood on the top stair. "Let us help, Sheila. We can put Charlie where he can't hurt you or anyone else. He's heading for a fall. He's dodged it until now, but he's in way over his head. Don't let him take you with him."

The sky had grown pretty dark by then. Not nearly as black as those eyes, and that's probably why I could see the moisture that glistened at their edge.

"I've known men like you, fella. And nothin' good ever came of 'em."

I wanted to reassure her, tell her that there were men who didn't want to hurt her or use her, men who could bring good into her life. She didn't give me the chance to say anything just then.

"There's one real important thing you haven't figured out, Sherlock. And that's what this is all about. I told you that earlier. Charlie may be a prick, but he's family. And that's why he's doing this. It's for us."

"What about the Klan?" Jamieson asked. "White Power and all that shit?"

Sheila wiped a tear away with the hand holding the Glock. In spite of the weapon and its caliber, it struck me as a pretty feminine gesture. She leaned forward on the stoop until she was inches from me. I could feel the heat from her body reach out and grab mine. I knew she had a presence. I had noticed that before. But I didn't realize she could capture me so easily.

"I don't care anymore. I can't speak for Charlie or Emma, but what I care about is family. And justice."

"But what's that have to do with the Burkhardts?" Jamieson pressed.

Sheila answered, but it was as though she hadn't heard him. Her words seem to drift right to me, and me alone. "He's the son-of-a-bitch that did this. He stole our land and killed my grandfather."

"And the church fire? Saints Peter and Paul?"

She drew back, and her eyes went cold. I had been released. "I don't give a damn about your church."

"But it's a part of all this, Sheila. We can't just forget about it."

"It's only the part you think it is. You need to do a lot more work, Mr. Detective."

"Then help me, Sheila."

She didn't answer. Those eyes returned and focused on me once more. I stepped back and started walking in the direction of the car, trying to break the spell. Her gaze never left me, though. "If you can't help us, you should just stay away."

"There's too much unfinished business between Charlie and me, between all of us. Charlie never should have dragged me into this."

"As I recall, you were in it already. He didn't have a choice." She paused to let her words sink in. "And I don't have one either. Not anymore."

Her stare held me for a moment more, then she disappeared back inside the house.

"Come on, Habermann," Jamieson yelled. "Let's go."

But before I had reached the bottom step I heard the screen door open and slam shut again. Sheila Harbour stood once more on the top step, a folded sheaf of papers in her hand. "Read this." She held them out for me. "It might help correct whatever that jerk Burkhardt told you." She paused and clenched her jaw. "He was a liar and a cheat. They all were."

Jamieson stood at the door of his Thunderbird, tapping on the roof with his knuckles. I was balanced on the bottom step, one foot already on the ground, but I couldn't bring myself to move any further. I wanted to stay to hear more about Sheila Harbour's grandfather and the Burkhardts. I kept thinking that if only I could get a little more information on the family's history, maybe I could pull all this together.

I also wanted to wait for that asshole Charlie Harbour. I still had a score to settle. But Sheila claimed she had no idea where he had gone, or when he'd be back.

Her voice broke through the frozen air between us. "When you do come back, you'd better be alone." She walked back into the house where her shadow hovered just inside the edge of the screen door. "This business goes no farther between us until you do. It won't help to have cops like your friend around. They haven't been able to do anything in the past."

I turned and trotted to the car. Jamieson was already parked behind the wheel and had the engine running.

"Why the sudden rush?" I asked. "You're the one who insisted on coming."

"I thought maybe you could use my help. I made a mistake. So I'd like to spend some time with my wife and kid this week. Besides, I'm already out on a limb here, Bill. It's not like I've got the authorization to pursue this thing on somebody else's turf. The local law could have Hardy fry my ass if they found out we were wildcating here."

I climbed on board. "Where was all this uncertainty earlier? Besides, I thought you and Peterson were old pals now."

Jamieson tossed the aggrieved teenager look right back at me. "How long do you think that will last if he catches us here? And this all seemed like a much better idea before we started. I'm not so sure now that I've seen her."

"What do you mean?"

He swung his head toward the house where Sheila Harbour had disappeared. "Her intensity is scary. Be real careful if, or when, you come back here. I think she's workin' to get her hooks into you."

"What's wrong with that?"

Jamieson shook his head. "You can be such a sucker.

Guys like us always think we can handle our women. Well, Bill...." He punched my arm. "I'm here to tell you we can't. So be careful."

Gravel spun across the blacktop as the Thunderbird pulled into the road.

"Point taken. I'll come back on my own tomorrow. I wanna look into property tax records as well."

"You're not even going to get close to anyone's tax records, Bill."

"You've been a cop way too long, Rick. Real estate records are part of the public domain. Now that I have an address I can request them as far back as I like. Or at least as far back as they go."

"What's the point of all that?"

I shrugged. "Depends on what I find. But if it helps fill in any gaps, it'll be worth the time and effort."

Jamieson dropped me off at my place when we got back to Naperville, and I dragged my butt up the back stairs, ready for bed. I didn't want to sleep on an empty stomach, though, so I grilled a ham and cheese sandwich, tossed a dill pickle and a handful of potato chips on the plate, and grabbed a Special Ex. After I flipped on the television to catch a Frasier rerun, I found the blinking light on my telephone. I dialed the message service and listened to the cheery tone of Alison Peterson.

"Oh, Bill, I just wanted to apologize once more for your less-than-hospitable welcome in our town. But I think you'll agree that it was a good idea, ultimately, to bring my uncle into your case. I can tell that he really likes you. And he has loads of experience in these sorts of things. So you can just let him take over from this end.

"If you do get to Morristown again, though, don't hesitate to stop by the Courthouse or give me a call. 219-646-0525. Maybe we can finally have that dinner. Bye."

A very odd message, I thought: an invitation and a kiss off. This was clearly a tough woman to figure out. But at this point I was too tired to try.

After another hour and two episodes of back-to-back Frasier, I cleaned the dishes, then aimed my tired ass for the bedroom. That's when I had another call from Indiana. And this one doubled the mystery of the women from that state.

"Hello, Bill? It's Sheila. I…I wanted to make sure you made it home okay."

"I appreciate your concern, Sheila, but my friend did all the driving."

"I'm not sure you should come back, though. Charlie's a dangerous man."

"I know that. That's one of the reasons I'm so concerned about all this."

"But he's also right in what he's doin'. Wrong was done earlier. It should be corrected."

"It's not up to Charlie to determine right and wrong, and not when he hands out the punishment. There are laws and courts, Sheila."

"They've cheated us before."

"Ray Burkhardt thought those same kinds of people cheated his family."

A sigh that spoke volumes drifted over the lines. "If you do come back, please be careful. I don't want anyone else to get hurt."

"You be careful, too, Sheila."

The pause that followed reminded me of how close and how far away she was. She hung up without another word.

Once I caught my breath I remembered the papers she had given me and trotted back to the kitchen where I had left them. I took the bundle, just a few pages, actually, to bed, where I propped my back against a couple pillows and read a brief statement, dated June 7, 1922 and signed by Randolph Harbour.

"I swear by Almighty God that Ray Burkhardt started the fire that burned down the Catholic Church in Naperville, Illinois out of malice for Catholics everywhere. I heard him state numerous times that he considered them unpatriotic and pagan, giving their loyalty to a foreign lord, the Pope, and trying to subvert our American way of life. He acted on his own, not on the orders of anyone else, or any organization. And to my knowledge, no one in the Klan ordered this burning. Ray Burkhardt claimed that the church in Naperville was an insult and that he was going to get rid of it. So help me God."

The second sheet contained a brief testament of sorts, this also signed by Randolph Harbour, but dated April 16, 1934.

"Before anything happens to me, I wanted to leave a clear statement for my family to urge them to rectify the wrongs that have been done to us. Quite simply, Ray Burkhardt cheated us. I'm not absolutely certain how, but he did. He may have spent those years in jail, but he still stole our property and the investments we needed to make our future secure. The wealth lies hidden, and only he knows where that is. I will not say anymore, only that it rightly belongs to the Harbours. Do not trust the law. They helped him steal it. May he rot and burn in Hell."

I couldn't read or concentrate anymore. Instead, Sheila's voice echoed in my mind, and I dreamed of dark-haired beauties all night long.

CHAPTER ELEVEN

So what? The statements gave the Harbours' side of the story, clearly one Sheila believed. But I had no way of knowing which side was closer to the truth. Or what the truth even was. Things were no clearer in the light of day. Not on this particular day, anyway.

The next morning I was back on that evil stretch of toll road, then down along I-65 to Morristown. These multiple tours on the World's Ugliest Highway were giving me all the inspiration I needed to bring the Harbours or the Klan or whoever was behind these killings to justice. I like to think I'm motivated by all the right principles and that I live my life according to the proper standards. But several things over the last few days had really ticked me off, and driving on the Illinois Tollroad was one of them.

I tried to smile, but it had been another tough ride. And those damn tolls didn't help. I still hadn't gotten the EZ-Pass for my car. I had waited until nine o'clock to let the rush hour traffic fade, but an accident had caused a four-mile backup. It was after lunch by the time I arrived.

Alison Peterson's face nearly fell to her waist when she saw me walk through the front door of the courthouse again. Her hands flew in the air, then settled on the counter. She was wearing a blue Oxford dress shirt over khaki slacks, and her hair was pulled back in a ponytail.

"I didn't think I'd see you again so soon."

"I thought your message said I was always welcome."

She bit her lips again, while the direction of her eyes darted from me to the floor, to the window, and finally settled on my shirt front. It was Madras, but not that attractive. "Well, my uncle will certainly be surprised."

"You'll probably be seeing me a lot more than you'd like. Or at least your uncle will."

"Don't tell me you're here being pursued by bad guys yet again. I wasn't aware we had so many criminals in this town."

"No, this time I'm just looking for the auditor's office to check some real estate records." I looked around. "I can always use the directory. If I can find it."

She sighed. "No, that's all right. I'm sorry. It's up on the third floor."

"Thanks. Can I get you a cup of coffee? Or maybe we can finally get that dinner afterwards." I had skipped lunch.

She smiled again. I was beginning to think it was a natural reflex for her. "No, that's okay. Nothing really good seems to come of you buying me things to eat or drink."

"Fair enough, for now. But maybe you'll change your mind when all this is over." I turned toward the hallway, where I saw the elevators at the far end. "I promise to fill you in sometime on how I saved all of us from a fate worse than death."

"Whatever. Just make sure you stop in to see my uncle. I don't think he trusts you."

"Did he say so?"

"Well, not in so many words." She paused. "Actually, he didn't say anything. It's just the way he's been behaving. Kind of stiff and worried. Just make sure you stop by if you do come back."

Great, I thought, another issue to deal with. I gave her a false smile, waved, then headed for the elevator that carried me to the third floor. I found the auditor's office to the right and halfway down the hall, lit by patches of electricity and sunlight. The walls and floor had that institutional look that comes with gray linoleum and plaster, although some of the building's history had been preserved in the elaborate crown molding that lined the ceiling. It seemed like everything in this state could use a coat of new paint. Except the Starbucks, of course.

There were two other people in the auditor's office, so I had to wait about five minutes for some service. A middle-aged woman, somewhere in her forties, I guessed, sauntered over to my spot at the counter, covered in a loose flowery shift that made a futile effort to hide a small mountain of humanity. I'm afraid I stared, trying to determine where the hips left off and the shoulders began.

"Yeah, you must be the one," she announced.

"Excuse me?"

"You the guy from Illinois?"

"I do live there. Why?"

"Alison called ahead to warn me."

"Against what exactly?"

"Bullshit. She said she could never tell how much of what you say is true." Blue eyes nearly hidden in liner studied me for a moment. "In my experience, it's the scariest parts that turn out to be true."

"What experiences are those?"

"Men."

I let that one go. After all, I did need her help. It bothered me, though, that I appeared to have a credibility problem with Alison, and possibly with her uncle. Now that someone had mentioned it, I realized I hadn't made many friends here at all. I was going to have to work on that, particularly since I figured I was going to need to have Chief Peterson on my side. But then, I had to admit that I knew next to nothing about Alison, her uncle, or anyone else here. I really had a lot to learn in Morristown. My attention drifted back to Ms. Mountain. "Well, this should be an easy one for you. I'm looking for the real estate tax records on the Harbour farm down along Route 41 near Clear Lake." I gave her the address.

"You want the property tax records as well?"

"I'm not sure what good that'll do. Do they own a lot of boats and cars and airplanes?"

She shook her head and snorted. "You Illinois people." Then she leaned her bulk over the counter, and the paneling seemed to groan under the weight of her breasts. "In Indiana, the property taxes are the records of a property's commercial use."

I thought of those full fields of corn and the Harbours' lack of any interest in actually doing any farm work. "Sure. I'll look at those."

"How far back?"

I hesitated. I hadn't thought that far ahead. "Let's say 1922." Her eyebrows arched. "The fire, dear. That's when Saints Peter and Paul burned to the ground."

"Where's that?"

"Never mind. I'll just take a look at the books."

By the time she had finished stacking tax records on the countertop, I was wondering if I would ever get out of Morristown again. The first patch that carried me through the 1920s, 30s and 40s weren't all that cumbersome. It was only in the 1950s, and even more so in the 1960s, that the area had really grown. But since I already had the address, I didn't have to spend too much time searching to find the information I needed.

According to the county records, the Harbours had purchased a 520-acre spread near Clear Lake in 1920. By 1937 it had shrunk to a mere 100 acres, which the family then rented out. Anyone familiar with the topography of our Midwestern states knows that they hold a lot of rich farmland, and northwest Indiana is no exception. It appeared that the Harbours had made ends meet by leasing other fields to farm until just before the Second World War, when the Harbours tried to expand their holdings. They were not successful. The property taxes listed a real fall in income from the farm, which never seemed to revive. At least not in comparison to some of the other listings. The family still owned the property, although it had shrunk to 50 acres by the early 1970s, which they again leased. They appeared to have given up on a life of farming around the same time.

I wasn't sure what all that told me. The sudden drop in acreage was interesting, but what about their lack of success as farmers? Maybe the Harbours had poor judgment in crop planting, although the land around here looked healthy enough to grow just about anything from what I had seen of it. And I hadn't noticed anyone growing much besides corn during my drives through the area. Maybe it was bad management, which would not have surprised me, given what I had seen.

"Interesting place down there," my hostess observed.

I glanced up to find my second favorite civil servant in northern Indiana standing right across from me. I wondered if everyone in this state was so silent. Maybe that's what made them such good basketball players. She must have noticed the puzzled look on my face as I tried to decipher the figures. "How so?" I asked.

"Well, the country down there has seen some real changes over the years."

"Like?"

"We call it 'Cleartucky' nowadays, for one thing. It's pretty much seen its better days fade and die." She wrinkled her nose. "Pretty much country-type folk now. You know, hillbillies."

"I see. But you say it wasn't always like that?"

She stood back from the counter, and her ample flesh shifted to find a new equilibrium. "Oh, Lord no. Back in the 20s it was a big gangster hideout. Those guys would come down there to build their private mansions on the lake and get away from the law back where you're from. It is across the state line, you know."

"Yeah, I noticed. There was a sign. But you say the area's fallen on harder times now?"

She nodded. "That's right. When Prohibition ended,

those guys didn't seem to need the place anymore. Besides, a bunch got busted. Some hung on for a while. But by the time World War II came along, those days were over."

"Is there anything there now to attract business?"

She shrugged, as though there wasn't much to consider. She gazed at the window to her left. I followed her line of sight, hoping perhaps to catch sight of a piece of history. But all I saw was bright sunlight and drifting clouds.

"Not really. The lake's dead from overuse." She must have recognized my puzzled look. "Nothing grows there anymore."

"From over-farming?"

She grabbed a small hill of tax books that seemed to bury themselves in her arms and chest. "I guess so. That and recreational overuse. Can't think of anything else down there."

"How'd it get a name like 'Clear Lake'?"

She started to back away. "Beats me. But it sure is ironic, ain't it?"

I thanked her for the local history lesson and left. On the way out, I nodded to Alison but didn't bother to stop. I decided to spare her anymore bullshit. Instead, I decided to drive down to Clear Lake. But I wanted to make sure the local law was aware of it.

Chief Peterson was back in his office. He was still in uniform, but his feet were propped on the desk, holding the corner in place now that the patrolman was no longer there. Smoke from a pipe floated toward the ceiling where it disappeared, while his gaze focused on the parking lot outside. A patrol car rolled to a stop, backed up, then angled into a parking space between two others.

"So, just what did you think you'll find down there at Clear Lake?" he asked.

I leaned against the wall and turned my face to peer out

the same window. I didn't find anything very interesting out there either. "Don't know. Hillbillies maybe."

"Come again?"

"The woman over at the auditor's office told me that's all that lives there now. She said it used to be a big gangster hideout, though."

"That was a long time ago." His feet fell to the floor. "That it?"

"Yeah. I'm just lookin' for inspiration. Kind of gropin' right now."

"You don't want to go down there to check on the Harbours's property?"

I approached the desk. "Their farm isn't at Clear Lake."

Peterson tapped his pipe on the edge of a glass ashtray, probed the bowl with a wooden match, then used it to relight the crust of tobacco left inside. "I'm not talkin' about the farm. They had some other land down there, but lost it back in the 30s."

"How much?"

"Oh hell, it must have been upwards of 200 acres. It was a nice spread. It was a ways off Clear Lake, though, up to the north. But they also had a nice lot on the lake itself."

"Were they gangsters?"

"Some think so. No proof, though."

"Can we see it?"

He stood and leaned forward through a cloud of smoke. "I figured you'd ask that. Any particular reason?"

I shrugged. "Just lookin' for inspiration, like I said."

He moved toward the door, and I followed. "Let's go. I should probably take you there so you don't get lost. But you're drivin'. I don't want to take one of my vehicles down there."

"Afraid of the hillbillies?"

"Shaddup."

It took maybe 20 minutes to reach the lake. I figured this was as good a time as any to clear the air.

"I don't think Alison likes me."

Chief Peterson shifted his weight in the passenger seat, adjusted the seat belt, pulled the visor down, then up, then down.

"You havin' trouble getting comfortable, Chief?"

"Hell, yes," he grumbled. "You mind if I smoke?" He waved a pack of Winstons at me.

"That's new. You didn't smoke cigarettes the other day."

"That's because Alison would've given me loads of grief."

"Help yourself then. But only if you can tell me some more about Alison."

He gave me a quizzical look, while the unlit cigarette dangled from his lips. "What do you care anyway?"

"Hey, our paths have crossed a couple times already. They're likely to do so again. I can't tell if she's with me, against me, or just doesn't give a shit. The woman's a real cipher."

Peterson lit up, rolled down the window, then tossed the match onto the side of the road. He drew the smoke in deep and held it, like a man who enjoyed his addiction. "They all are, son."

He pulled more smoke inside himself and seemed to use that moment to ponder my request before letting it drift out. "I'm not sure how much I should tell you. I mentioned the divorce and the dickhead she had for a husband."

"Was there another problem? Besides, the family thing, I mean. He sounded kind of rough. Did he abuse her?"

"With her uncle the chief of police?" He cracked a smile and looked at me, while more smoke exploded from between his lips. "Shit, son, the man wasn't a complete idiot."

"So, what was it? Does Alison date now, or has she

sworn off men?"

"Why? You interested?"

I glanced over. "I might be. You the over-protective type?" That got another smile, the kind that said don't push me. "What about her parents?"

"They're both gone. So, yeah, I am pretty protective." He studied me some more, then let his gaze drift out the window. "Cut the crap, son. If you want to work this thing out you don't need the complications Alison or any other woman would bring. So, let's just leave her out of it from here on in." He tossed the Winston out the window, and sparks bounced off the blacktop. "Okay?"

"Anything you say, Chief. We're on your turf here."

"And just make sure you and your buddy remember that. I don't want to hear about anymore solo trips by you boys to any farmhouses around here."

I stared at the chief, wondering what sort of network he had established over the years. I mean, it wasn't like Jamieson and I had cruised through town or anything. We hadn't stopped, except at the farm. We hadn't even pulled over to pee.

"Keep your eyes on the road, son." Peterson chuckled and shook his head. "What, you think we're just some country bumpkins?"

"Nope. But I still don't see...."

"Never mind. Just catch this left here."

Another half-mile and Clear Lake spread out before us in a smooth sheen of brown. The shore was lined with boathouses, once-impressive mansions, and a host of small one- and two-bedroom bungalows. We pulled into a parking lot next to a picnic area that had maybe a half-dozen parties working the grills for lunch and the open fields for some Frisbee and softball. The crowd was on the young side, teens and twenty-somethings from the lack of fat, plentitude of hair, and general stupidity as they drank and ran and laughed. I envied them. A couple speedboats shot across the water, leaving wakes of chocolate foam rippling toward the shore.

"Looks pretty dead. I don't see anyone fishing out there."

"It is dead. Like this town. Let's go."

"Where was the Harbour place?"

"Over there."

I pulled into the road and let the car drift forward for about 20 yards before parking next to a ditch that fronted a spread of oaks and poplars. Peterson was pointing to an open expanse of field that ran in a small hill up and away from the water. It was broken by half-acre lots with two-story homes of white siding and gray shingles. None of them looked like they had ever housed a gangster, or even one of his molls.

"Which one's their old house?"

"None of 'em. It was probably torn down years ago. What you got there are some vacation properties thrown up by a developer."

"Well, shit."

"What did you expect?"

"Not that."

He plucked another Winston from the pack on the dashboard. "Let's go. I'll show you somethin' else that might help explain some of this. Alison, too."

We rode back through Morristown, cruising through the downtown and heading for the northern limits. It lay just beyond the old city limits, the chief told me. Whatever it was. We cut across Route 55 and just north of 231 we aimed for a maze of new housing developments and apartment blocks. Peterson chose one of the latter that looked like a horseshoe of two-story, vinyl-lined, two-bedroom packages. The 'it' was three buildings in, maybe one hundred yards from the swimming pool and tiny clubhouse that looked like it could hold maybe 20 people, as long as none of them moved around too much.

I parked next to a pickup with a crib over the rear that held sets of ladders, each one chained to metal railings along the side with matching tools boxes—locked, of course. On the passenger side sat a battered white van advertising E-Z painters, Interior and Exterior, on the side panel. In fact, I would have guessed that about half the parking lot was occupied by vans and pickup trucks the occupants used in varying kinds of handiwork and labor. The rest of the spots were taken by a mixture of Nissans, Suburu station wagons, and an assortment of GM models, mostly Chevies, produced when Detroit still counted as an automobile producer.

"So what's here?" I asked.

"Alison's ex. His name is Wells. This could be interesting. Useful, too. We'll see."

We both jumped from the car at the same time and ambled over to apartment 218. The stairwell was clear, but the ground was littered with signs of children at play, mostly the brightly colored plastic vehicles and balls and bats that have made companies like Little Tykes a fortune. None were in use, though. I guessed the kids were at school.

Expressions in Vietnamese echoed in the stairwell, bringing me a momentary chill as memories from days long gone but never forgotten swept over me. I even stopped between the first and second floors for a moment, bracing myself with a hand on the banister. The stairs to the next floor seemed to sway in the afternoon heat, and sweat beaded along my forehead.

"You okay?" Peterson asked. He actually looked concerned and stepped toward me, his right hand extended to help.

"Just give me moment here." I brushed me face with my shirtsleeve and was surprised by a dark spot of moisture the size of my fist. "I'll be okay. Something just caught me by surprise, that's all."

A burst of Spanish washed the sounds and images away. Someone sounded pretty damn mad, and maybe it was the emotion in someone else's anger of the present that swept away my confusion from the past. In any case, I popped back to reality with Peterson's hand on my shoulder.

"Let's go," I said. "I'm actually looking forward to this."

Maybe it was my imagination, but I don't think Chief Peterson ever looked at me the same way again.

We knocked at a beige metal door that bounced in its frame. I wondered how much of a seal it provided during the northern Indiana winters. A man in his late 30s or early 40s in khaki slacks and a white v-neck t-shirt answered the door. His short, light brown hair looked like it could have used a comb, and his expression fell nearly to the parking lot when he saw Peterson.

"What do you want?" he grumbled. "I haven't seen Alison in months, so if anything's wrong on that front, you won't be able to blame me."

"Oh, hell, John, this doesn't involve her. We're actually hoping you can help us with some information."

"I doubt that. And you won't mind if I don't invite you in, I hope. I'm not exactly glad to see you." He finally appeared to realize that I was standing there as well. "Who are you?"

I gave him my name but didn't offer a hand. I figured I'd follow the chief's lead. Nothing hostile, but not much in the way of camaraderie, either.

"Bill here's from over in Illinois. He's involved in an interesting case that includes some of your old pals." John Wells didn't say anything to that, so Peterson ploughed on. "They are your old pals, I hope. And I seriously doubt you want us to chat about this out here on the landing where your neighbors could hear about it." Peterson halted to survey the neighborhood. "Doesn't quite seem like the right mix to me."

Wells still didn't say anything. He just stepped away and left the door open. Peterson and I followed him into what looked like a standard model: L-shaped living room and dining room combination on the left that wrapped around a small kitchen, bathroom straight ahead down a short hallway, with a couple bedrooms to the left and right of that. We moved no further than a set of chairs at the nearest edge of the living room and sat down.

"You not working today, John?" Peterson began. "Or is your new squeeze off earning the money while you play house dad?"

A crib filled with baby toys hovered at the far end of the room, just in front of sliding glass patio doors. Wash hung on the railing to dry in the afternoon sun. Towels and baby clothes, from what I could see.

"Don't talk about my family like that, Peterson." Wells looked at me. "Our chief of police is not a forgiving type. He can't accept that I left his niece for someone else when she became more trouble than she was worth. He doesn't seem to realize that we don't always control our emotional lives as neatly as we'd like. Or that in some lines of work you can have a more flexible schedule than a cop, which allows you to care for your family in different ways."

Peterson surveyed the apartment. "Sales must be off then, John."

"No thanks to you." Again, he turned to me. "I've had to develop an entirely new customer base outside the county since my marriage to Alison ended."

"Whatever," Peterson replied. "But you're wrong about the emotional part, John. You don't work as a cop as long as I have and not grasp something about what makes people tick. But there still is the matter of responsibility." He sighed. "Anyway, I wonder if you might know what Charlie Harbour's been up to lately."

John Wells grew visibly uncomfortable. He suddenly couldn't stay settled in his chair and refused to meet Peterson's eyes. He glanced over at me once, probably to gauge where I stood in all this. But then his eyes stayed with the carpet, the crib, the windows, anything but his visitors.

"I haven't seen Charlie or any of that crew in years. I'm out of it, and you know it."

"Well, I don't know it, John. Not for a fact anyway. How could I?"

Wells paused for a second. "Then you'll have to take my word for it."

I decided to jump in at this point. "Did he ever talk about his grandfather or the rest of the family?"

Wells lifted his gaze for a moment, as though he needed to register my presence. Seconds later his focus drifted away again. "Sure. Doesn't everybody?"

"But what did he say about 'em, John?" Peterson pressed.

John Wells shrugged. "The usual."

"Oh, come on, John. You can do better than that."

I intervened again. "What would the usual be for someone like Charlie Harbour?"

Wells shifted in his chair. "Shit, I don't know. I don't recall everything that was ever said."

"Did he ever mention someone named Burkhardt, or members of that family? Or perhaps a church fire in 1922?"

Wells lifted his eyes to mine and beyond. He seemed to be staring off into a distant past that grew closer the longer he hesitated. "I...I don't recall anything like that. Why would he talk about that stuff?"

"Because I think they mean a lot to him. There's been two deaths in Naperville, a town in Illinois. And we think Charlie Harbour's in the middle of it."

"And there could also be a shitload of money involved," Peterson added.

"How much?"

"It's hard to say," I answered. "We're not sure how much of the original sum is still around, or what was even done with the money. If it was invested, for example, it could be quite a sum today."

"Charlie still mixed in with those White Power creeps, John?" Peterson interrupted.

Wells finally met Peterson's eyes, then he looked off somewhere outside again. "I....I'm not sure. Some of those types hold on pretty hard once they get their hooks into you." Then Wells's eyes flashed, as though he had just remembered something. He looked straight and hard at Peterson. "I told you I wouldn't know. I haven't seen him lately."

"But you're the kind who would know if he is, aren't you, John?"

Wells's lips curled. "I was never in it that deep, Peterson. You'd know that, or you would, if you ever paid more attention to it. I got out as soon as I could. Right after I broke with Alison." His gaze drifted back to the window. "Either way, I wouldn't want to get cross with him or those others."

"Either way, John, we may need your help," Peterson replied.

Wells sunk back deep into his chair, as though he was trying to put as much distance as possible between himself and us. "What kind of help?"

"Give us someone we can talk to. Help us get closer so we can find out what's really going on."

Wells shook his head. "I've got a family now. I have to think of them."

"Yeah, I've noticed," Peterson said. "But helping us on this one would go a long way towards making things right again, as far as I'm concerned."

Wells' jaw set when he looked at Peterson again. "I don't owe you a fuckin' thing." He pasued for a second or two, just long enough to allow a new thought to arrive. "Did Alison put you up to this? Don't tell me she's involved."

Peterson's answer shocked even me. "I'm not sure, John. For all our sakes, I sure hope not." His own eyes followed the line of sight Wells had been pursuing for much of our conversation, from the rug to the window. "And, no, she doesn't know we're here."

I played along. "Remember, John, there are already two people dead."

"That's what I'm afraid of," he replied.

After a pause it became clear that we had gotten all the answers we were going to get. "I'll think it over."

"Don't take too long, John," Peterson replied.

When we got to the Cabrio I grabbed the chief's arm. "You mind explaining that remark about Alison? Just how do you think she might be involved?"

That deep, inexplicable smile crept back along Peterson's face. "Hell, son, I don't know where this is all gonna lead. Maybe I was just thinkin' of something to bring John Wells there over to our side."

I didn't believe him. I didn't disbelieve him, either. I didn't know anyone here well enough to be that certain of where they stood. But I did know that I was going to continue to play this one as a free agent.

I dropped the chief off at his station house, where he strolled in the front entrance between two patrolmen on a cigarette break. If it bothered them that they had to enjoy their vice outdoors while the chief used his office to smoke, they didn't show it. The two stood on either side of the door, both holding their share of the wall up with their shoulders and backsides. They straightened up when Peterson approached, then went back to sucking on their smokes and supporting the architecture as soon as he disappeared. They gave me only a cursory glance as I breezed from the parking lot back onto Main Street, oblivious to anything but their afternoon break.

At this point, I knew where I needed to go next, and I was going there alone. I didn't even bother trying to disguise where I was headed by aiming for the highway back to Chicago and then spinning suddenly southwards. Screw it, I figured. Peterson had pissed me off with his mysterious crap about his niece Alison, who, the more I thought about it, had inserted herself into this story and tried to push me aside. In fact, both appeared ready and willing to take over this case if I let them. I couldn't afford to play by his, or her, rules anymore. Besides, Peterson would find out anyway, sooner or later.

The late afternoon sun bounced off the Cabrio as I cruised south on Route 41, and the smell of mowed hay spread across the open fields. That changed momentarily to the aroma of manure when I got closer to the Harbour homestead, but that, too, had passed by the time I rolled over the sparse gravel in their driveway. I wanted another shot at Sheila Harbour while I had the opportunity, especially if there was a chance that her brother was not at home. I had to trust my luck on that last part, but her manner had struck me as an open invitation when we parted. And there was that call last night, when her words had drifted over the state line with a sound that reminded me of silk and seemed to carry a sense of longing. Maybe it was my imagination, but I just wish I knew where she wanted to take this thing. But I figured it had to be more, or certainly different, than I was going to get from the Petersons, or anyone else in Morristown. Right now, what I needed most was information, something more specific and tangible than some self-righteous and self-serving statement from Randolph Harbour. Or Ray Burkhardt, for that matter. And if it came from someone as attractive as Sheila Harbour, then all the better.

My luck looked to be holding. The LeSabre was still

gone, and the Explorer sat in the same spot by the kitchen porch. I pulled in next to it, jumped from the car, and jogged up the back steps. I couldn't find a doorbell, so I rapped on the screen door with the side of my fist.

"Come on in."

Sheila Harbour's voice did not have the strength or assertiveness I had noticed in our previous meetings, which I probably should have taken as a warning. I pulled the door open and stepped inside slowly. My antenna rose, since the atmosphere felt so different. I couldn't be sure if it was right or wrong, but at least it didn't sound like Charlie was home. I moved through the kitchen and found Sheila seated in the very chair in which she had wrung my ear just a day ago.

"Do you always offer such open-ended invitations like that to anyone who knocks?" I continued walking toward her as my eyes searched every corner of the room. Drawn shades blocked the sun, and the only light in the room came from a table lamp next to her chair.

"I saw you drive up."

I fell into the sofa across from her. "Through the shades?"

"I just pulled them now." A pause that seemed like minutes intervened. "I knew you'd be back."

"How so?" I noticed that Sheila had changed out of her jeans into a denim skirt that rode high on her thighs. She was wearing the same yellow cotton blouse, but I didn't care about that. Not entirely, anyway. She had a great set of legs.

"Because you can't help yourself. You know that I can help you, that I have more to give you." The glare from the lamp spread a warm, yellow glow across her thighs as she crossed her legs. She was reeling me in. I knew it, too.

"You're pretty sure of yourself."

She shook her head. "No, this is very difficult for me. I'm not sure I can trust you, or that you can help me." She smiled. "But I know what drives you. I have that much at least."

"And that would be?"

"The truth. Or what you think is the truth."

But it wasn't just the truth from where I was sitting. I shook my head to free it from the haze of her sexuality. It was starting to clog my thinking. "Is something wrong? You seem different."

Her hand rose and fell again to the arm of the chair. "I'm...I'm just not so certain anymore."

"About what?"

Her eyes drew me toward her. "Lots of things. Like my brother."

"Why don't you just tell me what you know, what it is that's really bothering you about your brother? Where is Charlie now?" She waved that off. "He's in the middle of this, Sheila."

"But he won't let you in. He'll only give as much as he needs."

"Then tell me what your family lost."

She straightened those legs and set both feet on the floor. Her arm snaked toward the window. "You see that land out there, the land you drove through on your way down here? That land belonged to us once. That and a lot more."

"All of it?"

"No, Bill Habermann, but the best of it did. The best of it was sold to developers, who turned it into all those shopping centers and movie theaters and gas stations."

"How long had your family had it?"

The arm fell to her lap. Her eyes burned suddenly with the fierce energy I had seen the last time I was here, nailed to the back stoop and enthralled by this woman, by her sheer presence. "Long enough. And we bought it fair and square, with money my grandfather earned."

"You mean the guy who burned my church?"

She leaned back in the chair and crossed those damn

legs again. I wasn't sure anymore if she was even remotely aware of where my eyes were focused, of how difficult it was for me to move. "I told you I don't care about your damn Catholic church. I care about my family and winning back what's ours."

It was my turn. I broke the spell and leaned forward. "So where'd Grandpa get all this money to buy so much land? Is that what ol' Jakob Burkhardt stole in the briefcase?"

She shook her head. "We already had the land."

"Then how'd you lose it?"

Sheila Harbour rose, smoothing the wrinkles from her skirt with long tanned fingers, then throwing her hair behind her shoulders. She stood in front of me like a piece of Greek sculpture, her hand stretched out to mine. It was an invitation I was not going to refuse, and she probably knew it. I stood up, and she circled both my hands with hers. Her face moved to within an inch of mine. She was so close I could feel the heat of her body. And mine wasn't exactly an ice cube anymore, either.

"Burkhardt stole it. I told you that already." Her lips brushed mine, while her eyes seemed to inhale me. I couldn't have moved if I tried. And I wasn't about to. "It's why my grandfather killed himself." Another brush of the lips, but harder this time. I brushed back.

This was news. It was certainly different from what was in the notebooks. I didn't want to lay all that out just yet. "But how? I thought he died in a car accident."

"He did it to himself, crazy with grief and rage."

She moved even closer. Her tongue slid across her lips to moisten them. The brush became a full kiss this time. Her hands squeezed mine hard. I may have groaned, but I don't remember exactly.

"That's what the briefcase was all about. It wasn't the money." More kisses.

I broke for some oxygen. "I don't follow. What about the

cash?" My knees had grown wobbly. "Can we sit down?"

Sheila shook her head, once, maybe twice. "Not yet." Her lips closed on mine again, and her tongue found its way to mine as she set another hook. "The cash was small change compared to the property. I need to find the original deeds. I think that's what was in the briefcase."

Her hands let mine dangle now, as her arms circled my waist and pulled me even closer. If that was possible. One of those wonderful legs hooked mine, and she moved in for another kiss, this one long and wet. If I had possessed the cash or deeds or anything of value I would have handed it all over in an instant, just to spend the rest of that day with her in that embrace.

"I'm sorry," I said, "but I don't know where any of that is."

"Well, you'd better hope you can find it," said a new and familiar male voice. The words were followed by a tunnel of steel, the kind you find on a gun barrel. It rubbed the back of my neck.

"I like the feel of your sister a lot better, Charlie." I still couldn't move. "In fact, I wish you were a million miles away from here right now."

"Well, I'm not. And I'm afraid you and I are going for another ride."

As I stepped away, I searched Sheila's eyes for some sign of regret, or longing even. But they had gone distant again, as though she could turn her emotions on and off as a matter of necessity. There was probably a good deal of regret in my eyes. I could only think of the lost opportunity to get so much closer to Sheila Harbour. Yeah, I wanted the information she had, information that I knew would help me on this case. But I was also certain she had many more mysteries to offer. I didn't care right then if she had set me up. I wanted to see her again and try to glean that information on my own. I figured I could handle that as long as I remembered what and who I was dealing with. Men do have a tendency to let our hormones do our thinking for us, instead of our brains. It's what gives us our false sense of confidence.

Thinking about all this on the way to the door gave me one more thing to add to my list against Charlie Harbour. I was definitely going to nail his ass to something before this was all over.

CHAPTER TWELVE

This time, Charlie Harbour had blindfolded me, so I wasn't sure where we were. I do recall driving east, or so it seemed once we hooked a left after riding south on Route 41 for a couple miles or so. In all, I'd say we had driven about 15, maybe 20 minutes. And it sounded like country all the way. Or to be more specific, the absence of sound had suggested country to my ears. And there was that smell of new-mowed hay mixed with the occasional whiff of manure. Ah, the farming life.

At any rate, we ended our journey in a trailer park of about a dozen vinyl-sided homes set on concrete foundations that gave the place an air of semi-permanency. Aside from a few decades-old Ford and Chevy compacts, the only vehicles that appeared to be allowed on the grounds were beaten and rusty pick-ups. One sat next to a white Chevy Impala in front of the trailer Charlie chose, where he ripped the blindfold off once we neared the steps.

"I don't want you to trip and sue me. My guess is that you can probably get a pretty good lawyer, seein' as who you been hangin' around with lately."

"I'd say your guesses aren't worth a whole lot."

"Well, in that case…."

Harbour followed this phrase with a shove that sent me face first into the door of the trailer. My nose stung from the sudden sharp contact, and a trickle of blood dripped across my upper lip.

"Thanks, asshole. I'll add that to the list."

His face started with a smile but quickly shifted into a leer. "Yeah, whatever. Just get inside."

That's when I saw John Wells. Imagine my surprise. He was seated at a small kitchen table covered in off white and gray freckles. The chair next to him had the padding creeping through a rip in the plastic covering at the back, but the one Wells occupied looked like it would survive the day. Someone else, the owner presumably, occupied the corner of a sofa set against a wall with light brown plywood for paneling that seemed to mark the boundary of a living room that began about five feet from where Wells sat. This guy was even heavier than Harbour and lots more ugly, with about a four-day beard that failed to cover a double chin and red-rimmed eyes. I doubted that came from lack of sleep. His overalls also failed to hide his girth, or the hairy shoulders. A shirt might have helped.

"So, what's up? You guys looking for decorating advice?"

Wells tried to catch my eye while he shook his head, as though to warn me. Mr. Sofa grunted, then looked at Charlie Harbour for orders. About a second later I felt Harbour's palm slap the back of my skull.

That did it. I spun on my toes and shot my right fist in the direction of Harbour's face. This guy was quick, though. Quicker than I had thought. He dodged to the side and answered my thrust with two quick jabs to my jaw with his left. I realized that a general boxing match would not be a good idea, and the cramped quarters in the trailer would only increase the disadvantage that came with his size. Considering that he had about 20 to 30 pounds on me, not one of which appeared to make him any slower, I wasn't sure that a grappling match was in my interests either. Still, I was so pissed I decided to go for it and lunged like a crazy bastard. I figured that was probably my best chance.

The Sofa Man made it all academic, however. I had managed to shoot inside Harbour's defenses and give him a good head-butt to the chin, when two fat, sweaty arms pinned my own to my sides. Great, I thought, not only will I get punched silly, but I'll have to take a couple showers to get this slob's smell off me.

Harbour, however, did not use his advantage. He dropped his fists and let the leer return. When he motioned toward the sofa, the oaf tossed me against the cushions, which smelled like last year's rainfall. Wells hadn't moved from his spot at the table. He stared at the floor while he massaged his forehead with a right hand that moved back and forth, as though to ward off the evil spirits in the room. Every once in a while, he peeked in my direction.

One of those times I caught his eye and asked, "So, who's sitting the kids?"

He shook his head some more and told me to "shaddup." I gave him a don't-blame-me look, and he finally responded, "The sister-in-law."

I turned to Mr. Bad Ass himself. "So tell me why the fuck you brought me here, Harbour."

He grabbed the chair with the torn cushion and gave Wells a playful jab on the shoulder. Then Harbour flipped the chair around and took his seat with the back facing me. Even more padding was drifting out the back now. The Happy Homeowner stood by the door at parade rest.

"I figured it was time we got down to some serious discussions, Habermann. And I wanted to do it in friendlier confines."

"Than your own house? What's wrong, Charlie, trouble on the homefront?"

The leer came and went. "Maybe. I'm not sure I can trust you around my sister. I guess it was a good thing I got there when I did."

"As I said, your guesses aren't worth a shit."

The Big Guy danced over and gave me a quick kick in the shins. I jumped up and when his hands flew in the air, thumped his chest. I hadn't thought about how his hairy, smelly chest would make my hand feel.

"Easy, boys." Then to me, "You'll have to forgive Harvey. He's got a sweet spot for my sister, which for some odd reason, she has never reciprocated."

"Imagine that." I sat back on the sofa. "So, what did you want to discuss?"

"Well, from what I can tell, you've been collecting a lot of information on my family. I gather you've bought the story about what evil men my grandfather and great uncle were, and you assume that they are at the bottom of this mystery."

"Where'd you hear that?"

Harbour chuckled. "You're not the only detective around here, Sherlock."

"You telling me they aren't?" I decided to hold back on the letters Sheila had shared.

"Ah, but there are others involved, and they bear a lot more of the blame."

"Well, those people haven't killed anyone that I'm aware off. There are, however, two dead men here."

Harbour tossed his hands in the air before letting them come to rest along the back of the chair. "Some things can't be helped. But more important to you would be some perspective on the players involved."

"Which ones?"

"The ones at the beginning. You see, my grandfather got his money the hard way. He earned it."

"From Smith and Barney?"

"Very funny. No, he earned it through his work with the mob."

"Doing what?"

Harbour let one of those goddamn smiles come back, then looked at both his partners before inclining his head to the side and looking over at me. "Let's just say he performed favors that were richly rewarded."

"Very cute. I'm sure that would relieve him of having admitted to anything in a court of law. Which gangsters were these? The ones living around Clear Lake?"

"Well, it appears you have learned something useful down here. That's right. It's why he took up residence there."

"Is that how he could afford such a nice piece of land?" Harbour nodded. "That, and more."

"What did that have to do with the Klan?" It may have been my imagination, but the Homeowner by the door seemed to stiffen when I used the K word. Wells just stared at me.

"Absolutely nothing. My grandfather was never in the Klan."

"And your great uncle?"

He smiled again. "Well, that is a little different. There were rumors to the effect that a political connection of some sort to the KKK helped my great uncle win office up in Morristown, but when the Klan's power faded in the state, he was able to survive because he had never been a real member."

"I'm happy to hear that. But how does this revelation help me understand things better?"

"Well, I don't want you to leave Indiana without understanding exactly what it was like back then for the people involved. And I don't want you to go back to Illinois without understanding what sort of people you're representing back there."

"First of all, I'm not representing anyone, Harbour. I'm only interested in justice for two dead people."

That got a guffaw from Harbour and the Fat Guy. "Give me a fuckin' break," the latter said. "Charlie, lets dump his ass in the lake."

Harbour's hand rose, as though to still the troubled waters. "No, he needs to go back. The police in both states know where he is and where to look should he disappear, at least while he's our guest. It's unfortunate that he's involved, but I think the best thing here would be to send him back so he can bow out gracefully. That's why I'm tryin' to explain these things to him."

"So just what was it like for those poor people way back then?"

"Times were hard, Habermann, and people made do, but those who stole from their own kind were no better and in some cases a lot worse than the others."

"Meaning?"

"Meaning that the thief who ended up with the treasure was even less deserving."

"What else do you have to say?" I pressed him.

"That you should remember this: Money is nice but land is more important. And when someone has had theirs stolen, then it's only right to want it back."

"So, you're trying to tell me that the murders are justified by your claim to some land allegedly stolen decades ago?"

Harbour slammed the edge of the chair. "Goddamit, Habermann, I told you it was stolen, and it was that bastard Burkhardt who took it!"

"So, how'd he do it?"

"It was all in the fucking briefcase, you idiot." Harbour shut his eyes, and his forehead furrowed in a grimace that made it look like he had lost his place or forgotten something. "At least there was something in there that would explain where it all went and what it was worth." Another grimace. "Or make all this worthwhile. I'm sure of it."

"No, Harbour, your sequencing is confused. Burkhardt had the briefcase, which he was supposed to give to your grandfather for burning the church down...."

Harbour jumped up. I followed suit, not wanting to increase my disadvantage in size and numbers.

"Why would my grandfather burn a Catholic Church, you dipshit? He had been working with those wops from Chicago for years. Think about it, goddammit."

"Then who did, and why did Burkhardt have the

briefcase?"

"Burkhardt was tried and convicted...."

"On your great uncle's testimony."

"....And a lot of other evidence as well. I'm telling you, Burkhardt was in the KKK. My grandfather was not."

"But if he had been some thug for the mob, he would have been a perfect person to turn to when you wanted a church torched."

"Only if he was a freelancer."

"Well?"

"Check the records."

"I already have."

"Well, check them again."

"Fuck you. I've heard enough."

Harbour strode right up to me. His fist shot out and grabbed a hunk of my shirt. "Listen shithead, you're going to hear one more thing before you go. Check the records back in Illinois. Then don't come back. If you do, I'll kill you."

"You aiming for a nice hat trick, Harbour?"

His grip tightened, and his right hand drew back. There was a moment's pause. I waited for the proverbial shoe to drop, wondering how I could work myself around behind Harbour to gain some leverage and hold Fat Boy at bay. But then the fist fell to his side, and Harbour's eyes got hard with hatred. They were the eyes of a man who could commit murder as easily as I crossed a street.

"John," he said, "give Mr. Habermann a ride back to his car at the farm. Harvey and I have some business to attend to." He turned back to me. "You get to leave because it serves a purpose, Sherlock. This is your chance to keep your Illinois friends out of things over here. You have no idea how this can shake out. And believe me, none of us, not a single person you've met, wants you here."

Wells rose from the chair and walked to the door. His

shirt clung to his back in a wave of wrinkles. I looked into and then past Harbour's eyes, and the fright I had experienced when we first met returned with the realization of just what this man could and would do. Oddly, I thought of his sister at that moment. I had the feeling there was at least one person who did want me to help.

"Tell Sheila I'll catch her later," I said. "We have a conversation to finish."

Fat Boy lumbered over again, but I was ready this time. I moved in his direction, then hooked my leg behind his and threw my arm around his big shoulders. He dropped to the floor, where his body bounced off the dirt and dust on the linoleum. A deep grunt escaped from a mouth buried in folds of flesh and whiskers, and then a string of obscenities poured from between yellow, crooked teeth. I looked at Harbour and let my own smile creep in. Not a muscle moved in that face. I backed slowly toward the door and down the steps outside, where Wells stood waiting next to the Impala.

"I thought you said you were out of it."

Wells didn't bother with the blindfold. Not that I would have let him. We rode in silence for about five minutes. My sense of smell had been accurate. We passed fields of alfalfa and rows of corn on the way back.

"Your friend in there seems a bit confused on who did what to whom and what he expects to find," I said.

Wells shrugged. "Maybe. That's his problem. But I am out of it. Have been ever since I left Alison."

I sat forward. "Then what were you doin' there?"

Wells glanced in my direction before turning his eyes back toward the road. "I set the meeting up, Sherlock."

"Why?"

"Because I thought it was the best way to avoid another killing. No one's going to get out of this thing any other way."

"What way is that?"

Wells paused while he chewed the inside of his lip. "I had to let Charlie try to talk you off this thing. I thought it might give you an opening to get out of it."

"You didn't think I was about to drop it, did you?"

Wells shook his head. "Suit yourself. At least I tried."

I pondered his remark for a moment longer. The smell of manure drifted back into the car, so I rolled the window up.

"What was that comment about Alison? You said something about having been out of it since you left her. What's that got to do with anything?"

Wells laughed out loud, then held his grin while he shook his head. "She and the chief really have you snowed, don't they?"

"What do you mean by that?"

"Hell, man, she's the reason I got involved in the first place."

"Say what?"

"That's right. She got me involved in all this crap. She's a real throwback."

"You mean she's a racist? I never would have figured her for the bigoted type."

"Oh, and just what are they supposed to look or act like?" More head shaking.

"Well, shit, I don't know. But still...."

"Anyway, she isn't a bigot. Not in that sense. I mean, her attitude on race isn't what some liberals would like, but it's a lot better than it used to be. Besides, it's Catholics she hates. Or used to, anyway." He studied the road and thought for a moment. "Maybe hate's too strong. It's more like she never really trusted them." He sighed. "In any case, I'm not sure where she stands anymore. It's been a while."

"Jesus, Wells. Who even gives a damn about that kind of thing anymore?"

"Look." Wells's hand rose from the steering wheel, then

147

dropped to the seat. He blew out his breath and shook his head some more. If he kept this up, I was afraid he'd make himself dizzy. "Alison was raised in the Missouri Synod wing of the Lutheran Church. They are really conservative, and many cannot stand the Catholic Church. You always hear all this crap about the corrupt papacy, like we were back in the Middle Ages or something."

"You telling me they're all ready to burn churches?

He shook his head. "No, nothing like that. But Alison is the type to go overboard."

"So, she joined the KKK."

The hand flipped up and down again. "Listen, there is no KKK. It's not that they're aren't some sympathizers with that stuff, but there isn't any organization to speak of anymore. Certainly not like before."

"Then what is Alison's story?"

"She was wandering around the right fringe, basically looking for something to belong to. She latched on to some white power guys briefly. I think that's how she got to know Harbour. I met him through Alison."

"Are you saying her religion drove her there? Are all these Missouri Lutherans like that?"

"Missouri Synod, dickhead. And no, they're not. As far as I can tell, the Church would never condone anti-Catholicism and certainly not violence. I think it was just the first thing Alison latched onto. Her own thinking drove her further to the fringe."

"Is she still involved with right-wing groups?"

"I don't think so. Like I said, it's been a while. And I always suspected it was more of a nice-girl-attracted-to-bad-boys kind of thing."

"Is she still involved with Harbour?"

"I certainly hope not."

"Is Chief Peterson aware of all this?"

Wells shrugged again and looked out the driver's side

window. "I'm…I'm not really sure. I think he knows some of it. But I doubt he's aware of how far in she once got."

We'll see, I thought. We'll see about that.

Wells pulled into the Harbour driveway and dropped me at my car. "Charlie Harbour is one mean son-of-a-bitch," he said. "Don't think Peterson can protect you. He may be able to find Charlie if something happens to you, but it will still happen. You'd best go back to Illinois and stay there. Besides…."

He paused to study the dashboard and the horizon.

"What is it?" I asked.

His hand roamed over the top of the steering wheel. "You really should stay away. There's a lot of history here, and it complicates how the people fit together."

"I'm not following you."

He turned to look at me. "I can't warn you to watch your back, because you won't see anything. Nothing's how it looks. Leave it to Peterson and your own cops. They'll take care of it. At least they're the best chance for real justice."

"That sounds strange coming from you."

"Don't let my case fool you. That isn't what it appears to be either. Just stay back in Illinois. We don't need more death around here."

"That's the way I feel, too." I studied his face for a moment. "Anything else you want to tell me?"

Wells actually smiled. "Look, I don't know anything about a briefcase, the Klan, the deaths you've been talking about, or any of that stuff. I just know the people involved. You don't want to be there if this all goes south."

I climbed from the car, then leaned back inside before I shut the door. "Thanks for the ride," I said. Then I threw the door shut.

When I turned toward the house, I saw Sheila standing at the window. Screw John Wells, the Petersons and Charlie Harbour, I thought. I've got unfinished business with his sister.

Sheila Harbour turned and walked away from the kitchen window the minute I walked through that back door. I quickened my pace and caught her in the living room at nearly the same spot we had occupied when her brother interrupted us. I grabbed her arm, just above the wrist, to make her stop. Sheila wheeled to face me, her eyes wet with the tears. I was stunned. Confused, too. I hadn't thought she was capable of any sign of weakness or vulnerability. And I was even less sure than before of where she stood in all this. She pulled her arm free and continued to stare, first at me, then deep down inside me. She rubbed her arm where I had held her, as though she wanted to erase a memory.

"Why'd you come back? I thought you'd be gone for good."

"Would you like me to leave?"

She nodded and started to speak. But then her lips closed and worked themselves against her teeth.

"Well, too bad," I said. "You were the one wrapping her legs around me, roaming my face with your lips."

"Is that why you came back? For some more of that?"

I took her arm again and pulled her closer. It was my chance now to turn on the charm. What little I had. I glanced at the floor before finding her eyes again. Small streams ran down her cheeks. "Yeah, okay, I liked it. I liked it a lot. But it won't work. I need to know why you set me up."

"I didn't set you up. Charlie wasn't here when you arrived. Did you see his car when you came in?"

"Then what happened?"

"He snuck in and neither of us heard him. I didn't think he'd be back."

"Why not?"

"Because the police are looking for him. This is probably the first place they'd try. I thought they'd have the place

150

staked out."

"So, what do you want from me?"

Sheila pulled her arm free again. It's not like I was holding it real tight anyway. Her hands roamed along my upper arms. "I want you to help me, to help us."

"Us? You really think I can reclaim that land?" She didn't answer. "You should try a lawyer, if that's what you're really after. I don't think they believe in sex, though."

"No, it's not just the property. It's more." She chewed her lower lip.

"Stop with the mysteries, Sheila. If you want my help, you're going to have to come clean and tell me everything. What does 'more' mean?"

"It means I want you to help me."

"How?"

"Help me get free."

"From what?"

"From this. From my brother."

"I thought you wanted to get your family land back. That sounds to me like you plan to stay stuck right in the middle of this mess."

Her hands moved up over my shoulders and found each other behind my neck. "That's how I can get free. I need to get this settled."

"Give me Charlie. We need to make sure that no one else is hurt, Sheila."

She took a step back from me, then another, her head shaking back and forth. "No. It's not that simple."

"Damn it, Sheila, I know he's your brother," I said, much too loudly. "But you can't protect him. It will make you an accessory."

Sheila's head shook some more, then stopped when she clasped her hands together in front of her chest. "No, that's not it. Charlie may be involved in the killing at that house in Naperville. But he didn't kill that Burkhardt guy. I'm sure of it."

"How?"

"Because he was here that night. He read about the murder in the paper."

"Which one?"

"*The Tribune*. We get that here, too, you know."

"So, why did he go to Naperville?"

"He said something like 'It's back on.' Charlie said he needed to act fast."

"Fine, then let's go to the Station and you can give them a statement."

Sheila Harbour stood silently and nearly still for about a minute. It felt a lot longer. Only her head moved as she studied the ceiling, the windows, the floor. Anything but me.

"Okay," she finally said. Then she moved in closer. Her hands fell to her side, and she raised her head. The tears had dried, and before I knew it she was up tight against me. "Tomorrow. We'll go together."

"Why tomorrow, and why do you need me?"

"That's the only way I'll go, Bill." Her lips found mine again. "And I need you to stay here tonight with me."

Her tongue wet my lips for me. I was a goner. I knew it, and she probably knew it as well. Against my better judgment and that of males everywhere, I asked her why.

"Because I don't want to be alone tonight. And I want you to be the one with me." She paused. "And because if you don't, I'll lose the courage to act."

"What about your brother?"

"I told you, he won't be back. Not for a while anyway. He needs to avoid the police. They came by earlier with a warrant."

Her breasts pushed against my chest, and her hands ruffled the hair along the back of my skull. My knees felt like they were made of putty. Still, I forced myself to ask one last question.

"What is it, Sheila? I know you're not doing this because I'm so pretty. What do you really want?"

"Only partly because I think you're pretty. I know you'll help me, because I know you like me. And you want to bring all this to an end."

She took my hand and led me to the stairs. She was right, of course. I did want all this to end. I knew that was the only way I could find the killer or killers, and make sure no one else got hurt. Sheila included. And even if that wasn't the case, I didn't really care at that particular moment. I followed those legs up the stairs, convinced that I was in pursuit of one truth or another.

CHAPTER THIRTEEN

It was the sun that woke me this time, not the noise. I did hear something, but only after my eyes broke open in the middle of a blaze of white light. I rolled away from the window to shield my face and found Sheila lying on her side, her face toward the wall and away from the sun. It seemed as though she was trying to hold off the outside world and all the trouble it held. I propped myself on an elbow to get a closer look at her face. The soft ebb and flow of her chest suggested that she was still asleep. The closed eyes, too. Remember, I'm a detective.

I studied the full, dark form that lay beside me, and one of those warm feelings you read about spread inside me. This was something I knew I could get used to. True, Sheila struck me as a real beauty, but her body, hell, everything about her spoke of mystery and longing that pulled me deeper into a place where I wanted to be but wasn't sure I belonged. Then I remembered the darker side of that mystery, the history she carried so personally, and so dangerously, into the present.

I rolled over and slid from the bed to take a leak. I slipped on my boxers, then paused by the window. Oddly, there were no curtains or window shades, which explained the early morning blaze. Thankfully, there was no Le Sabre outside. Just the Explorer and the Cabrio. The noise I had heard must have been squirrels from the patch of forest that ran east in the direction of Ohio, starting about one hundred yards from the house. Or perhaps it had been the pigeons. Lord knows they tend to congregate in barns. I had shot enough with my brother and friends as a kid back on the farms surrounding Naperville.

When I returned to the bedroom, Sheila was sitting up, her back against the bed frame, the sheet drawn to her waist. A smile spread under eyes soft with sleep; it made her face look warm and welcoming. As I approached the bed, she tossed her hair back over her head and shoulders so that it rustled like silk shrubbery. Her breasts swayed in sunlight that had suddenly gone soft with shadow.

I fell on the mattress beside her and gave her a long, slow kiss. I didn't want to move. She seemed to enjoy it, opening her lips and putting a lock on mine that sent a shiver down my spine and all the way to my toes. She kicked the sheet to the foot of the bed, pulled my boxers free, then rolled over on top of me, pinning my hands to the mattress. Those wonderful legs wrapped themselves around mine again, and I felt her moist, bushy warmth as she straddled me until we were both ready. Her nipples turned hard, and she took me inside her. I lost myself in a world of bliss and lust while the sun shot streaks across our bodies.

Afterwards, we both lay moist and sweaty, our arms and legs spread across the mattress. I propped myself up on one elbow again. "What's with the windows?"

She rolled toward me. "What do you mean?"

"There aren't any curtains. I can see why you don't need to worry about the neighbors, but doesn't the sunlight bother you in the morning? Especially in summer when the sun rises so early."

"You wouldn't be referring to this morning, would you?" She smiled again. My heart moved several inches.

"Well, yeah."

She shuffled her body closer and pinched my neck with her lips. "This isn't my normal room. So I never really paid attention."

Only then did I realize how spartan the room looked. No wall hangings, nothing atop the dresser, no clothes strewn about. Nothing to give it a sense of personal ownership.

"Geez," I exclaimed. "So what's the story? Where's your room?"

She pointed at the floor, beyond the bed. "One floor

down."

"Then why are we here?"

She pulled away and propped herself on an elbow to mirror my position. "I wanted someplace new for us. I wanted a room untouched by anything else in this house and its history."

"You mean like Charlie, in case he came home?"

Sheila leaned away and climbed from the bed. "No, Bill. I mean like I wanted a space for us alone. You and me, and nothing else, if only for a night."

I didn't know how to respond to that. Beautiful and mysterious, Sheila Harbour had gotten me to break one of my rules of the trade: never, ever get sexually—and certainly not emotionally—involved with someone on a case. It had happened once before and had nearly cost me my life. I told myself that this would be different, that I would stay in command, since I knew Sheila had her own agenda. Besides, like most males, I figured I could keep my distance emotionally and sort through all the byplay to get the information I needed. Now Sheila was showing signs that this could mean more to her than either of us had anticipated. And she wasn't alone. It always sounds so much easier than it is. I climbed from the bed and headed for the shower, hoping the hot water and steam would make things clear again. They didn't, of course.

By the time I got downstairs, Sheila had made coffee, and a plate of scrambled eggs and bacon was waiting for me at the kitchen table. Steam curled from a white mug next to it. Sheila was washing dishes in between sips from her own ceramic mug from the Indy 500.

"You still want me to go to the police station?" She wiped the countertops with a moist green washcloth.

"I think that's best, Sheila. We need to assemble all the pieces to figure this thing out."

"It's just not as easy as you might think."

"Well, you need to show your head's in the right place if you hope to avoid an accessory or obstruction charge." She just stared at me over the rim of her mug, those deep, dark eyes piercing my chest. Goddammit, I thought. She is either very smitten or one damn good actor. I wasn't sure at that point which one I preferred, or which one I could deal with better. "Besides," I added, "it could possibly help your brother."

She set the mug and dishcloth down next to the sink. "Then let's go. I'll stop on my way to work."

"I'll follow." I placed my dirty dish and fork in the sink. "I need to check in with Naperville after."

Sheila looked at me, her eyes suddenly blank, and shrugged. "Whatever."

I reached out and pulled her to me. I studied those eyes until they softened a bit, then kissed her slowly and deeply to let her know I planned to return. One way or another I was coming back, and she needed to know that. Her hands found my arms and squeezed hard enough to bruise.

At the station, we were ushered into Chief Peterson's office by the patrolman I had met on my first day there. Stale smoke hovered in the sunlight by the windows, and Peterson glanced up from a stack of paperwork the moment we entered.

"Well, well. If it ain't the odd couple."

"What the hell's that supposed to mean?" I protested. Sheila just gave him one of her stares. It had a lot less effect on the chief than it usually did on me.

Peterson tossed a silver fountain pen on his desk blotter. "Oh, hell, I'm sorry. I didn't mean anything. It's just that you two are not the people I expected to walk in here together one morning."

"You should be happy we did, Chief. I convinced Sheila to come in and make a statement. I understand you guys have a warrant out for her brother."

Peterson stood up and walked to a filing cabinet behind his desk. He pulled out a middle drawer, reached inside, then slammed it shut. He returned to his desk holding a tape recorder. "We don't," he said. "Your friends in Naperville do. We agreed to apply it if we could find Charlie. It's only for the death of a two-time loser named Bert Haggerty." He looked at Sheila. "The name mean anything to you?"

She nodded. "I've heard it before."

"I'll bet you have. And?" Peterson continued.

"I don't recall meeting him, so I can't say anything else."

"She claims her brother was with her at home the night Burkhardt was killed," I added.

"Well, your pals in Illinois may agree. Or at least they haven't found any evidence to indicate otherwise. We'll see what we come up with here."

Peterson stared hard at Sheila for about a minute, glancing over at me periodically. Then he motioned toward a chair in front of his desk. He turned the machine on, spoke the time and place, gave the names of the people in attendance, and so on. After Sheila waived her right to a lawyer, she told Peterson the same story she had given me. She also claimed that she had no idea as to Charlie's present whereabouts, and that she hadn't seen him in roughly 24 hours, the last time being when he had returned to abduct me at gunpoint. She left out the words 'abduction' and 'gunpoint,' however. I didn't bother to correct her, as I wasn't really interested in filing a complaint.

"Anything else you'd like to add?" Peterson asked.

Sheila and the chief exchanged another set of hard, almost brittle stares. Maybe it was my imagination, but I could have sworn the temperature in the room rose about ten degrees. Then she refused to say any more without a lawyer present, as though she had suddenly gotten wary of the entire proceedings.

When she finished, Sheila rose and walked past me to the door. Her hand brushed along the back of my skull, and she gave a tight, sharp yank at a tuft of my hair. She paused just long enough to take the chief and his office in one more time, her hand holding a fistful of my hair the whole time, pulling my head backwards in her direction. Then she hurried from the station without another word, as though she couldn't escape the torture chamber quickly enough.

Afterwards, I tried to give a description of the trailer park to Peterson.

"Could be any number of places," he said. "It sounds like it's still in the county, though, so I'll let my friends on the county force know."

"What's the story on the Haggerty guy?"

"That's actually kind of interesting," Peterson replied. "Ol' Bert appears to have been quite active on the white-power, neo-Nazi scene. He'd had a number of priors, some of 'em violent. Assault and the like."

"Sounds like it fits the earlier pattern."

"Which one would that be?"

"The one about the money coming from the KKK and the push to retrieve it. That's the one we started with anyway."

Peterson smiled. "Is that the one you're going to stick with, son?"

I stiffened. "I'm not sticking with anything. I'm still gathering facts and learning about the characters." I didn't fill him in on all my interactions with the Harbour clan, which was creating a much broader, and personal, story. "Do you think this Haggerty guy could have killed Burkhardt?"

"Oh, hell, anybody could've killed Burkhardt, based on what little we know. What I find the truly interesting question is why Charlie Harbour saw fit to kill Haggerty. Doesn't that make you wonder what's goin' on among those creeps?"

I admitted that, yes, it did, although I told the chief about Harbour's version of the 'accident.' Then I got up and left for home.

Before I reached the highway, though, I thought I'd visit Sheila at work. It wasn't so much that I missed her already, although I did like the idea of perusing the dirty movie shelf with her. What I really wanted to do was ask if there was any kind of history between her and Chief Peterson. That eye duel she had had with him earlier made me wonder if there was a more personal connection between them that I needed to understand if I was ever going to get to the bottom of this Burkhardt-Harbour business. Was this one of the personal cases that John Wells had warned me about?

I was parked in my car in a bank parking lot to the left of the video store across a side street and was pondering just how I should phrase my questions, when I saw a bronze Pontiac Bonneville pull into the store's rear lot. The car model looked to be about 20 years old, but the body sparkled with enough polish and sunshine to make it look brand new. Not a speck of rust, or dirt for that matter.

Chief Peterson hopped out and marched inside, where he stayed for all of about five minutes. When he strode back out, Sheila Harbour trailed in his wake. He spun around and spoke to her, his face pink with rage, veins rising in streaks along the sides of his neck like small snakes. Sheila stood there, her arms folded in front, trying to freeze him in place with one of her masterful stares. I was proud of her. When she shook her head, though, he reached out and grabbed her upper arm. She tried to jerk free, but Peterson held fast. I started to climb from the Cabrio. Then, just as suddenly, he unclenched his grip, then ran his hand over his forehead and through his hair. Sheila rubbed her arm where he had held her, and I wondered if the bruise I had seen before had indeed come from her brother.

I sat half-in, half-out of my car and rolled my window down to see if I could hear any of their argument, and even shout to distract Peterson, if necessary. But he wheeled toward the Bonneville, climbed on board, and roared off in a blaze of summer light and dirt, a cloud of brown haze drifting in the air where he had been. I guess police chiefs don't have to worry about speeding tickets. I gave up on pressing Sheila for information on her and the chief under the current circumstances. I probably should have gone in to talk to her, to try to console her, but suddenly I felt very unsure of my own position in the constellation of characters in this town. I wanted some more time to think things through.

About a mile from the Illinois border I found the same bronze Bonneville sailing up on my tail. It was dirtier now, mostly dust and grime from the toll road. Before I had time to figure out what Peterson was up to, he had a blue light flashing on his dashboard, while he waved me to pull off to the side of the road. Peterson rode in behind me, leaving about four feet between our cars.

Trucks and vans and sedans breezed past on our left, and it seemed that all it needed would be for just one to swerve and tumble us into the yawning chasm that stretched into the sky over the abandoned quarry to our right. I crawled out on the driver's side, then inched my way back to Peterson like I was walking on a tightrope. He already stood with his rear parked on the grill of his Pontiac, his arms set across his chest like armor.

"Where'd you get the wheels, Chief? The boys back at the station keep it in shape for you?"

"Don't give me any of your fucking banter, Habermann. I want to know just what's going on between you and Sheila Harbour."

"Easy, Chief. We're both of consenting age. And I never did make a play for your niece."

"Grow up, asshole. I don't care where you put that dick

of yours, as long as it doesn't screw up an investigation in my town."

I leaned against my trunk. "Shit, Chief, I thought I actually helped. You think you would've gotten that much without my persuasiveness?"

Peterson peeled himself from the Bonneville and came to within inches of my face. I could smell the mints he used to cover the tobacco on his breath.

"Listen, cocksucker. There are things in this case you will never understand...."

"Like what?"

"Like never fucking mind. That shit this morning was the last straw."

"Then stop shutting me out. Give me what I need to get to the bottom of this."

"The bottom, as far as you're concerned, is the Naperville murder. And your friends are taking care of that. Otherwise, you're off limits, Habermann."

"Jesus Christ, Chief, you sound like you're trying to protect someone. And from what I saw back at the video store, it wouldn't appear to be Sheila Harbour. Or would it?"

Before I took my next breath thick, meaty fingers had circled my chin. The pressure pushed in and up, as though the chief would have liked to separate my face from my neck. "Easy, Chief," I squeaked. "You're on thin blacktop here. There are plenty of witnesses."

"None of whom give a damn, Habermann. They're in too much of a hurry to get someplace else. And that's what you're goin' to do."

"You're not runnin' me off that easily."

"I saw your car in that bank lot, Habermann, and I'm just glad I got to Sheila before you could have caused any more trouble. Keep drivin' west and don't come back. You can keep track of things through your friends on the force."

"What if I don't follow your orders?"

Peterson freed my face and turned toward his car. "Then throwing you in jail would be not only a pleasure, but a public service. At least you'd be alive."

At that moment, a semi rolled by with enough force to shake me into another time zone. The highway actually shook underneath us. It didn't make Peterson or our conversation disappear, though. In fact, it seemed to push him back closer to me, where I saw sunlight shine on cheeks red with anger and eyes scarlet with rage.

Then I remembered his grip on Sheila back at the video store. My own anger rose to match his. "As long as we're making threats here, Peterson, let me warn you to keep your fuckin' paws off Sheila Harbour. You grab her again for any reason, and I'll break your neck." I stopped to catch my breath. "I don't care what you call yourself, Chief."

The color in Peterson's face faded. He even grinned a little. "Just what are you after here, Habermann?"

"I would have thought the same thing as you, Chief. Justice."

"Oh, shit, son." He winced. "You don't know fuck all about justice. If you hadn't crossed that state line, none of this would have happened." He blew out a breath of stale air that smelled like worn asphalt. "You proud of yourself now?"

"I don't know enough to be proud about anything involving this sordid affair, Chief. But I do know I didn't start this thing, and I didn't ask to have this tortured history resurface on my watch."

"You still pushed it, son. That's why the blame rests with you now. And I want you to leave that right where you found it."

"And that would be?"

His finger pointed straight down. "Right here."

"And if I don't?"

"Then you'll be responsible for what comes of it as well."

Well, I did know that was bullshit. I just shook my head. I hadn't started that fire, fueled it with hate and greed, and then let it simmer all these years. I wasn't a perfect, or even a particularly good catholic, and maybe my sins were coming back to haunt me now. It had happened before. The sisters had even warned us about that kind of thing back in school. But I wasn't the only one facing that dilemma right now.

I inched my way back into my driver's seat and sat for about a minute, studying Chief Peterson in the rearview mirror. Then he climbed back into his Bonneville. He followed me to the state line, then caught a break in the railing to pull a U-turn and drive back to Morristown.

Back in Naperville, I stopped first at my apartment to check the mail and the phone messages, stir up the dust, let the flies out for a walk, and so on. There were two messages on the phone from Rick Jamieson wondering where the hell I'd been, along with a voice mail from my good friend Jamie Krug over in Oswego. I made a mental note to get together with Jamie as soon as this case sorted itself out, then left a message for Rick at the office and his house to tell him I was back in town and would swing by later in the day. Of course, it was already afternoon. I flipped on my window air conditioning unit in the living room, then bolted down the back steps for the garage.

The mid-afternoon traffic in Naperville surprised me with its density and pace. I had figured on maybe 15 minutes, tops, to get from my place to the library, but it took me 40. And the cause was nothing more than the unrelenting growth that continued to change the very nature of my town. In this case, the volume of traffic guaranteed a slower pace that meant you hit every traffic light as it changed before you had the chance to get through the damn intersection.

I was hoping for better luck at Nichols Library, but the parking lot was full. I finally found a space three blocks away on a residential street with non-resident parking limited to two hours. When I barged through the doors, my favorite 1960s retread was working the help desk, but she had traded her baggy denim shift for a pair of pleated slacks and a light, cotton pullover. She looked almost bourgeois. But the ponytail and granny glasses blew her cover.

"I was wondering if I could ask one more favor through your library loan program."

Ms. Librarian set her hands on the counter and gave me a smile that made me forget all about the traffic. It was so nice to meet a friendly person just when I was prepared for the worst.

"Of course. What can I do for you?"

"I need to check the Illinois Klu Klux Klan membership lists for the 1920s. Is there some way we can retrieve these?"

"I think so." She grabbed a notepad and pen from where they had been resting on the countertop, wrote the letters "KKK," a dash, and then "Illinois." The smile was still there when she looked up. "What was the timeframe again?"

"Oh, let's say 1910 to 1930." I wanted to be safe here. "That should do it. Are there records available for that kind of thing still?"

"I believe so. Or there should be. I can contact the Illinois Historical Society in Springfield. I don't know about police records, but we wouldn't have those in any case."

"Probably not," I guessed. "I don't think the KKK was illegal here then, and I doubt the local records would have survived anyway." I had tried once before to get some local police records from the years before World War II and discovered there were none.

She picked up the pad and pen again. "Let me see what I can find. If the Society has anything, I can probably access it on their website or get them to send me an attachment."

I thanked her and promised to stop by again before they closed.

"Oh, we're open late tonight. I'll be here until eight o'clock."

Now that, I thought, was service. It made me glad I paid my late fees.

By then it was about three o'clock, and I realized I was pretty hungry. I pulled into a Subway and bought one of those foot-long cold cut sandwiches but decided to skip the chips and soft drink in favor of a beer at home. Then I figured I'd call Jamie Krug and apologize for falling out of touch over the last few weeks. I never got the chance, though.

Oh, I made it home all right. I even managed to eat my sandwich and down a beer. But Jamieson and Hardy were waiting for me in my kitchen when I arrived, and they kept interrupting me with a host of intrusive questions. That bumped any phone calls I wanted to make to the bottom of my to-do list.

"If I keep finding you clowns in my apartment I'm going to start charging rent. You ever heard of an American citizen's right to privacy and protection from unwarranted searches?"

"Does sound vaguely familiar," Rick Jamieson replied.

"Try the Constitution," I muttered. "Look under 'Amendments,' somewhere near the top."

"So call the Supreme Court," Hardy said. "Or better yet, hire a private eye."

"Hardy, har, har, Hardy." I smiled and pointed my finger at him. I had just thought that one up.

"You've been hard to find lately, Bill," Jamieson continued. "We thought we'd better wait for you here."

"Now, why would you guys be looking for me?"

"Chief Peterson tells us you've been spending a lot of

time in Indiana," Hardy pressed. "You wouldn't be keeping any secrets from us, would you?"

"That depends, Frank. You been keepin' any from me?"

"Like what?"

"Like the Burkhardt shooter. Here I've been working on the assumption that the same killer is responsible for both deaths. Then, lo and behold, I find out you guys have got a warrant out for the second murder only."

"Which we understand you found testimony to support," Rick added.

I nodded while unwrapping my sandwich. "That's right. Charlie Harbour's sister Sheila claims she can place him in Indiana the night Burkhardt was shot."

"Can anyone vouch for her whereabouts?"

That one threw me. "Which night? Burkardt's killing? If she can place her brother at home, then she must have been there as well."

"Says who?" Hardy pressed.

I decided I'd better move very cautiously here to avoid tripping over my own story, which suddenly sounded a lot more complicated. And suspicious. I stood up and walked to the refrigerator. "You guys want a beer?"

"What's the matter, Bill? All that late night research got you thirsty?" A wide shit-eating grin split Hardy's face.

"What's that supposed to mean?"

"It means you've let your dick lead you on this case, which also means I no longer trust your judgment."

"If you ever did." I couldn't offer much more of a protest, since I realized how suspicious this all looked. In his place, my response would have been the same. I strolled back to the table with an Augsburger for me and one each for my uninvited guests.

Hardy leaned across my kitchen table and grabbed the beer. "Oh shit, Habermann, we both know we don't like each other...."

"Speak for yourself, Frank." Those words escaped between bites of my sandwich. "I just gave you a beer."

"See, that's just it," Hardy continued. "You're a smart ass. Always have been and always will be. You're more interested in scoring funny points than doing your job. Oh, you're honest, all right. But I never know just how far I can trust you. And that's why I don't like working with you."

After that little speech the local police chief drained about half the beer in his bottle. I guess stringing all those sentences together at once had made his throat dry and his brain tired. I looked over at Jamieson, who put down his bottle and shrugged. He was used to these confrontations. About a third of his brew was gone. These guys must have been waiting a long time. I was surprised they hadn't helped themselves.

"Does this mean I don't get to learn what you all know about the Burkhardt shooting?"

"There's not much we can tell you, Bill," Jamieson said. "Can anyone vouch for Sheila Harbour's whereabouts that night?" He went back to his beer.

"And there's even less we'll tell you now," Hardy added.

"You know, Frank, it's just that sort of bullshit that makes me hate working with you. I'm the one who's been pursuing leads in the Harbour family, and I'm the one who brought the sister over and got her to give her testimony."

"And we appreciate that, Bill," Jamieson interrupted. "No one's questioning your integrity, or your help."

I continued like I hadn't heard my best friend just try to build a bridge. "And I had planned to stop by and fill you guys in as soon as I got back."

"Which you didn't do," Hardy said, before sucking on some more beer.

"I wanted to get something to eat first and check a hunch at the library. But apparently, Frank, you expect me to come and genuflect at your desk first and deliver my news on bended knee. Well, fuck you. That's not gonna happen." I bit off another chunk of sandwich.

"So, okay. Give us what you got," Hardy said.

I chewed slowly, my eyes on Hardy. "You first."

"Why?"

"Because it's my house." I nodded at his bottle, which was empty now. "And that was my beer."

He and Jamieson exchanged glances, their eyes darting back and forth. Rick retreated behind his nearly empty bottle. Beer foam slid down the inside of green glass.

"You guys playing I-got-a-secret or are you coordinating prom dates?"

Rick Jamieson spoke up. "There's nothing conclusive, Bill."

"But?"

"Whoever it was may have ridden with Ray Burkhardt for a while. We found traces of fabric in the car that we'd like to match."

"What kind of fabric?"

"Cotton and cashmere. And some make-up."

"Interesting combination. Was the make-up smeared somewhere?"

"The back of the seat."

"So you think it was a woman?" I thought of Burkhardt's behavior at the Lantern. "And you think the killer was able to get in his car by pretending she was interested in some romance?"

"Why do you ask that?" Jamieson pressed.

I reminded them about Burkhardt's antics at The Lantern. "It wouldn't have been very difficult."

"Have you wondered why they were on Diehl Road?"

"Yes, but I haven't thought of an answer, unless they were going to park for a quickie."

"Not a real good location," Hardy suggested. I didn't

answer. I was too busy trying to think of anything I had seen Sheila Harbour wear that might resemble cashmere. I came up blank. Then again, I had been too busy to check her closet, although I didn't tell Hardy and Jamieson that. "Can you be sure she was in the car that night?"

"Not really. And we aren't even sure we can link the evidence to the shooting. But the ballistics and the wound suggest the shooter was real close. Like in the passenger seat."

"And then had someone drive her, or him, away?"

"That's right. There were tracks indicating another car had been there. But this stuff only helps if we can get a suspect."

I looked over at Hardy. "Maybe that explains Diehl Road."

"How so?"

"Close to the Tollroad. A quick getaway."

"Yeah, back to Indiana."

I was pretty quiet for a minute or so, pondering that one. I figured they would soon have Peterson test the tires on the Explorer, if they hadn't already. I told them about my own adventures in the Hoosier state, but I left out the sleepover with Sheila, which no doubt disappointed them, and my confrontation with Peterson. I was pretty sure they knew about the Sheila Harbour escapade already from Chief Peterson, and I wasn't sure what I should say yet about Peterson's strange eruption, so I gave them a brief outline. I hadn't figured it out myself yet.

After they left, I finished the sandwich and Augsburger, rinsed the beer bottles and dropped them in my recycling bin on the back porch. Then I drove to the library before it closed to see if that list of Illinois Kluxers was ready. It took 45 minutes this time, but I did find a parking spot in the lot near the street.

A gentleman in a light gray cardigan (probably because

of the air conditioning, which was blowing pretty strong) that matched his short hair and trimmed beard sat alone at the information desk. I figured him for a retired school teacher or something. I gave him my name and asked if anything had come in for me.

"Yes, I believe so." He searched the shelves underneath the counter between us. I could hear paper and packages being shuffled. "Yes, here it is."

He popped up with a manila envelope in his hand. "Yes, Sarah put your name on it. She had to go home, I'm afraid."

"Thanks so much." I took the envelope. "And please thank Sarah for me."

This time I couldn't wait until I got to the car. Instead, I walked over to one of the reading tables by the windows, sat down, and pulled the paper free. It was indeed a print-out from the Illinois Historical Society, about a dozen pages long. The Society had apparently faxed the list to the library. Fortunately, nothing had been smudged or lost in the transmission, and I was able to read all the names clearly. When I saw the name, my heart sank. My jaw with it.

Jakob Burkhardt had indeed been a member of the KKK. He joined in 1912 and remained a member in good standing until 1923, presumably because he couldn't pay his dues from prison.

I didn't really look for any other names. So it was pure luck when I saw it. And I couldn't be sure he was any relation. But it seemed an Oskar Peterson had also belonged to the Klan here in Illinois, and he had lived in Aurora. He joined in 1915 and stayed a member right up until the Klan was outlawed in 1938.

CHAPTER FOURTEEN

This discovery certainly set me back. Not all the way to the beginning, but almost. I sat at the table in the library for about half an hour, thinking back to the notebooks and Ray Burkhardt's testimony in my office and at the Lantern that first night. How much of it was credible now? I no longer doubted there was some sort of hidden treasure at the root of all this, as well as disputes over land, inheritances, and debts owed somewhere. But how all this fit together and what Jakob Burkhardt's and Charlie Harbour's claims to the treasure were, and where the responsibility for the fire that destroyed Saints Peter and Paul back in 1922 fit in were no more clear than before.

Then I remembered that some time ago I had wondered if Burkhardt had had an accomplice waiting on the outside. It would have been his only way of insuring that the bundle from the suitcase had stayed put, if he really had buried it in the forest. He couldn't put all his trust in Mother Nature. Who was this Peterson guy? It wasn't a common name, but not an unusual one either. Was he related to the chief? Had Peterson been that confidant? If so, what had become of the treasure and him? Or was this just complete conjecture, just some wild guess based on coincidence? It was clearly a stretch, but then what else did I have?

It took me another 30 minutes to peruse the list of local Klan members to see if any of the names from the area jumped out at me. There weren't many. And none of them sounded familiar. There were a couple more in Aurora that I figured I'd have to check out as well. I wasn't sure yet just how, but something would occur to me. Hopefully.

But first I decided I needed to do something else, something here in town that would help me find new evidence to shed light on where the real connections ran. So I drove through the late afternoon Naperville traffic, framed in fading sunlight as it crawled along Washington Boulevard south toward the sea of new housing developments that had multiplied and spread across the Illinois farmland like a flood. And it wasn't going to recede anytime soon. Not with the way the local economy was booming. If anything, the development had reached a new stage. I tried to outflank some of the traffic by cutting through the residential section downtown, and I passed a few of those new multi-million dollar mansions that barely fit inside the property lines. One friend, the owner of a plumbing company, claimed that some of those things held as many as seven or even eight bathrooms. I guess once you got rich, one advantage you gained was not having to walk very far to use the can.

At any rate, I was not aiming for any of those new palaces, nor the new housing construction along the city's southern boundary. I left the big "tear-downs" behind and cut around Naperville Central High School and the acres of little league and softball fields just south of that until I entered Moser Highlands from the back, turned onto Gardner Road, then drove toward the DuPage River. I cruised past the Burkhardt home on Edgewater, twice, in fact. The police had long since disappeared. Or so it seemed. I gathered that they had concluded there was no more evidence to be found there. Crime scenes rarely stayed closed off for all that long anyway.

On the second pass, I continued past the house for about a hundred yards, then pulled over to the curb under a stand of about half-a-dozen oaks. Those trees had marked the right field wall during our home-run derby games as a kid, but now they'd have to provide some cover for my Cabrio. I pulled a flashlight from the glove compartment, locked the doors, and ambled back to the house still rimmed in yellow tape.

Obviously, I wasn't going to let that stop me, so I marched

up the driveway and around to the back. The time, however, the local law had remembered to lock the door. I played with the lock for about 15 minutes, then lost my patience. I wrapped my fist in a handkerchief from my back pocket and punched out one of the small, square window panels. It was the one above the door handle. Not a smart move, I conceded, but the ugly new developments and lack of sleep were beginning to affect my mood and judgment. To make it easier, I pretended it was the face of Charlie Harbour. After cleaning the shards from the frame, I reached through and undid the deadbolt and handle lock. If anyone asked, I'd blame it on vandals.

Of course, I had no idea what I was looking for. I had already sorted through every room in the place looking for missing chapters in the Burkhardt saga. So I wandered the hallways, foyer, rooms and basement again in search of inspiration.

It came when I was upstairs. In the hall, to be precise. The outline of an attic door stood out clearly against the surrounding ceiling space, highlighted by a ray of light from the master bedroom window. There was no rope extending from the hook at the end, so I figured that must have been how I had missed it the first time. Maybe the cops had as well. Maybe not. But I was going to have a look anyway.

First, I tried a chair from the dining room downstairs, mostly because it was easy to carry up the stairs. But it left my fingers about half-a-foot shy of the hook. Next, I pushed a dresser from the guest bedroom into the hall after pulling out the drawers to make it lighter. This worked just fine. Except that when I lowered the door, the ladder couldn't extend all the way because the dresser was in the way. So I left the door propped open, pushed the dresser back in place, retrieved the chair, and pulled the ladder all the way down.

The hot, stuffy air hit my face like a wet towel straight from the sauna. I had to pause for a minute or so to let my body adjust, or try to adjust. It never really did. The sweat started to drip from my forehead and cheeks almost immediately. I searched in vain with the flashlight for a ceiling fan, but then decided I'd just have to suck it up. Within minutes, the moisture was rolling down the back of my neck and small puddles formed along my forearms. I had been in saunas before but remembered them as a lot more enjoyable than this.

I used the beams along the floor as my walkway through the space to see what sort of treasure the attic held. There were piles of old books, laden with dust and the musty scent of ancient paper, most of them Readers Digest condensed bestsellers and school textbooks that spanned decades. There was probably a living history of American education sitting there. A few pieces of old furniture, bedroom sets from someone's childhood, and boxes of old photographs filled additional space. I thumbed the latter for familiar faces—or even a resemblance—from the last few days but came up empty.

At this point, I decided I needed to dry out. I climbed back downstairs and wiped myself off with a towel from the bathroom. I figured to hell with forensics. I had left enough traces of my presence as it was. So I took the next logical step of grabbing a new towel and returned to the attic with it.

At the northern end of the attic I found several book boxes bound with packing tape. They were the last things left to be explored, so I ripped the tape back and pried the lids open. Inside each box sat bundles of correspondence and a few more photographs. The first box contained letters between Ray Burkhardt's parents, as well as letters the son had sent home from various wanderings around the United States and Canada. Yes, I felt like a pervert reading someone else's personal correspondence, but I was desperate.

In the second box I found letters to and from Jakob

Burkhardt. There were several dozen exchanges with members of the Harbour clan, principally old Carl Harbour's brother during and immediately after his tenure as the Morristown mayor. There were also exchanges with the next generation of Harbours, some of them pretty intense after Burkhardt's son and his wife—Ray's parents—died in the car crash. And there were accusations as well about the Harbours' role in that, followed by some bland denials, noticeable for their lack of conviction. That's how it all read to me, anyway. And there were letters to and from the most recent crop of Harbours, young Charlie in particular. He was not a very literate man, but he did appear to be knowledgeable about history. Certain aspects of history, that is, and principally his own interpretations.

Clearly, the families had stayed in touch. Not with affection, or even friendship, mind you. But they knew where each other lived, and they had continued to argue their respective cases down through the years. Suddenly I realized why Ray Burkhardt had brought his case to my door that night, and I had a pretty good idea what he had been looking for and why he had died. I was less sure of who had done it, but the respective roles of the characters in this decades-old drama were a lot clearer now.

Had Ray Burkhardt known about these letters? He might have, and he may have been prepared to tell me of their existence, if he had lived, even if they did throw doubt on the veracity of his granddad's notebooks. But he had obviously been spooked enough by something to reach out to someone he thought could help, or even protect him. And I had failed. Of course, he hadn't been exactly honest, as best I could tell. What was still really unclear to me was what, if anything, had happened to whatever was in that briefcase. Maybe I'd be able to answer that one once I figured out whether old Jakob had had an accomplice, and who it might have been.

I repacked the second box and pushed it back against

the wall where I had found it. I was tempted to take the lode with me, but I didn't want to taint further potentially valuable evidence. Sure, Hardy would have had my ass, not to mention my license, but I also did it for the principle of the thing. I raised the ladder and attic door, replaced the furniture, and tossed the towels in the tub.

On my way through the dining room the telephone rang. Now, that struck me as really odd. I was tempted to lift the receiver to listen for a voice, but I also knew that I didn't need to take any more chances than I already had. If I had answered, though, I would have known who was calling. And he was trying to reach me anyway.

It was time to call Jamieson. He and Hardy had been playing bad ass with me earlier, but I knew that my best chance of finding out what they really had was to speak with Jamieson alone. Fortunately, when I called he was home. His wife Susan answered, and she grabbed her husband.

"Okay, Rick, tell me the whole truth," I said. "Or the real truth."

"Pardner, we were as square with you as we could be. Under the circumstances."

"Meaning?"

"Meaning your dalliance with the suspect's sister...."

"Whom I brought around."

"Yeah, well, we'll see. You need to be sure you're not thinking from your pants on this one, Bill." I heard Susan scold Jamieson in the background.

"So you really expect me to be satisfied with that crap about angora sweaters and silk threads and mascara? That's a public defender's wet dream. What else have you got?"

"Well, there is the angle of the shot. Ballistics thinks the shooter was slightly shorter, which points to a woman, or a dwarf."

"That from the angle?"

"Yeah, maybe."

"Very clever, Rick. But that's not very convincing either. The shooter could simply have been someone sitting lower, or bent over. You need to be even more obtuse. None of this implicates Sheila Harbour. You've seen her, and you've seen her wardrobe. She's at least as tall as Burkhardt was. So piss on the angle thing. Tell me why I should stop seeing her."

A pause followed. It was longer than usual. I even had to ask Jamieson if he was still there.

"Goddammit, Bill."

"Eventually He will do just that to the guilty parties, Rick. But I'm trying to bring them to justice in this world first."

"Shit, I knew your stupid love-life would result in something like this." Another pause. "You remember the tire prints we mentioned? I told Hardy not to bring them up?"

"The ones Peterson is supposed to check?"

"We lied. He already did."

"Go on."

"They match her Explorer."

It was my turn to pause. I could feel my heart pounding through my chest like a turbine gone haywire. "How long have you known this?"

"Since yesterday afternoon. Right before we came to your place. It's what had Hardy in such a funk."

"So it was after I had Sheila give her statement."

"I guess so. Why?"

"Has Peterson pulled her in?"

"He said he was going to go looking." Maybe, I thought, that explained the confrontation at the video store. But then why had he just left her there?

"It doesn't mean she was driving." I knew this was lame, but I was groping.

"We'll see about that, Bill. But it does raise questions about her claim that her brother Charlie was with her that night."

"True." I started to think. Or, at least I tried to. I mean, this really threw things out of whack, and just when I thought I was beginning to figure everything out. Against my better judgment I had let that woman get inside my head and heart. I thought I had kept everything in their proper compartments, but in that moment I realized I had been fooling only myself. Now I had to determine whether my judgments had been clouded on other aspects of the case.

"Boys," my mother used to say, "always have more hormones than brains." Even mothers can be right sometimes.

But my mind wandered again to why Peterson hadn't pulled Sheila Harbour in and what was behind their argument at the video store. Had he known then, or even earlier, and not told Jamieson? But then, why play all the drama in taking her statement? Because of where they were, at the station? And why jerk me around?

"Bill? You still there?"

"Yes, Rick, I am. But not for long."

"What's up?" Now he paused. I could hear him breathe out sharply on the other end of the line. It was almost a hiss. "Shit, don't do it, Bill."

"Don't do what?"

"Don't go running back there. Let Peterson handle it."

"No can do, Rick. I'm not sure that's the best option either. He may have his own agenda."

"You know something we don't?"

"Not sure just yet. Probably nothin', but maybe somethin'."

"Listen, asshole...."

But I hung up before he could finish. I hurried to the bedroom to retrieve the Baretta, just in case. Then I remembered that I had left it in the car, in the locked glove compartment, of course. On my way out the door the phone rang. I considered just leaving it ring, assuming that it was Jamieson trying to re-establish contact. And I already knew what he was going to say. But on the off chance that it was someone else and also important, I picked the receiver up. For once, I was right.

"Well, well." Charlie Harbour sounded so pleased with himself he was almost singing. "Finally reached you, Billy-boy."

"I'm glad you called, Charlie. We have some unfinished business."

"You sure got that right. I've been trying to reach you all day. I even called Burkhardt's place. You seem to like it there."

"What's so fucking important from your end, asshole?"

"Now, now, let's watch the language. Sheila would not approve."

"That's one of the things we need to settle."

"You got that right," he warned. "In fact, that's what I want to talk to you about."

"You going to give me some of that big brother crap?"

"No, I wasn't planning to. Although I can if you'd like."

"Get to it, Harbour."

"No, in fact, Sheila's here with me now. And actually, I'm upset with both of you."

"Why is that?"

"Because she turned against me. I heard about your visit to the police department today. That tops even her bringing you into her bed, Habermann. Although that sure as hell says something about her poor taste in men. I guess she's been down on that farm too long."

"How'd you hear about our visit to the police?"

"Oh, I have my ways. I also have my ways of paying off

debts."

"She spoke in your defense, asswipe."

"But she still talked to the cops, like you wanted. That opens the wrong doors. And that has to be fixed."

"Just what did you have in mind?"

"If you don't get your ass down here with what I want in 24 hours, Sheila is dead."

"You sick piece of shit, Harbour. She's your sister."

"Not anymore. Once you give me what is mine, you can have her."

"How do I know you've really got her there?"

"You wanna talk to her yourself?"

A rustle at the other end of the line followed. Then Sheila's voice came across the wires. It did not sound good.

"Don't, Bill, he's crazy. He'll kill you anyway." She yelped as a thud echoed over the phone, and then Charlie Harbour's voice returned.

"You've left quite an impression, Billy-boy. You must be a good lay."

"We'll see who gets in the last crack, you prick."

"Twenty-four hours, Habermann. I'll be in touch. As soon as you give me your cell phone number, that is. And no fancy tricks with your cop friends in Naperville. If I suspect anything, then Sheila dies early. And I come looking for you."

"You won't have to look very hard."

I gave him my cell number with a curse and a promise.

CHAPTER FIFTEEN

So I had the better part of a day to figure something out. It was already late into the night, the sky as dark as my mind. Jamieson and his colleagues among the local law were not much of an option. And Peterson? That had to be where I started tomorrow.

I set the alarm for six and was on the road to Aurora by seven. Traffic was heavy, of course, since I had put myself in the middle of a local rush hour on one of the principle east-west routes, Aurora Road, which becomes New York Avenue as you enter Aurora. A patchy sky painted a ceiling of alternating blue and white to match the shopping centers that dotted the landscape between the two cities. It didn't seem all that long ago when I had encountered open vistas of cornfields and pasture, broken only by an occasional farmhouse and patches of woods, and the movie screen from the drive-in theater along this road. My friends and I had tried to sneak in to watch Elizabeth Taylor in Cleopatra once. I had had as much luck at that as I was having with Charlie Harbour.

I arrived at the library five minutes before it opened, but it took me another 15 minutes to find a parking space. The information desk inside was just as helpful as ours in Naperville, and within another 20 minutes I was seated at a reading table with a set of city directories that took me back as far as 1947.

And there was indeed an Oskar Peterson residing on the east side of town back in 1947, on Union Street, to be exact. I consulted a city map and found his block just to the south of Galena Avenue. That put Peterson's Aurora residence near the center of town. Of course, I couldn't be sure it was my KKK man, but he was the only Oskar Peterson listed in this directory, and the only one still residing in Aurora, according to the stack on my table that went up to 1957.

Then I checked the other names. There had been five others on the list from Aurora, but only two had addresses in the city directory at the time. One name disappeared after 1929--something to do with the Depression perhaps--and the other was gone after 1933. I gambled that neither one had been in cahoots with Burkhardt since they were no longer around when he got out of jail. Of course, they could have moved somewhere else nearby, but I did not have the time to check every burg in DuPage and Kane counties. Then I remembered the list of Klan members out in the car, which I could use to verify their departure once I left the library.

I gave back the pile I had, grabbed another armful and returned to my table. The city listings continued to hold the name of Oskar Peterson until 1962, when he sold his house to someone named Walter Jefferson. According to the directory, Oskar had also worked for the city until his departure. The directory did not contain his position or job title, however, just the employer.

Thinking back, I seemed to remember that this was a neighborhood that was heavily African-American. I guessed that if this really was the KKK man, then he may have left when his neighborhood had gone from largely white to predominantly black. That was only a guess, though, as I had no idea what Aurora's demographic history was like, or even Oskar Peterson's personal history. And if he was indeed my man, where had he resettled? Someone his age—I assumed he retired—normally headed south, not east to the border with Indiana.

All this still left me a long way from any kind of confirmation that the Chief Peterson I knew had emerged from a family in Indiana that had originally come from Illinois. And even if I did confirm that, then so what? The sins of the fathers do not automatically transmit to their sons (or grandsons), and Chief Peterson had never done or said anything to suggest that he agreed in any way with the tenets of the Klu Klux Klan.

I was obviously groping. But I felt a little better when I saw that none of the other Aurora names were still listed with the Klan after the 1930s. This was not rock solid proof, of course, but I did feel a little bit better.

I decided to call Jamieson again despite our troubled conversation from the night before. Fortunately, I had my cell with me. He was at the office when I reached him.

"I'm surprised you called in," he said.

"Rick, I'm always happy to talk to a friend. Besides, I could use a favor."

"Fat chance, pardner. I hope you haven't done anything stupid already."

"Not yet, but it's still pretty early. Tell me, though, what do you guys know about Peterson's background?"

"Enough to know he's a good, solid cop. Why? You got problems?"

"Not really. I'm just trying to run some stuff down. Is he a native Hoosier?"

"I think so. At least he attended school there. Criminal Science at Butler University. Worked there all his life, too. What's up?"

"What about his family? Do they go back generations there?"

"You looking for one of the original settlers or something? We all come from somewhere else, eventually. We're Americans. Remember?"

"Is there any way you can check for me? Official records or something?"

"Why not ask him yourself?" Rick snapped. "You know him well enough already."

"I'd rather he didn't know."

Jamieson blew his breath into the phone. "Come on, Bill. What gives?"

"Humor me, okay? I don't want to suggest anything that may be off base and end up smearing the name of a good cop."

"Dammit, you'd better not be off base here. I'll see what I can do. Where can I reach you?"

"I'm running a bunch of errands this morning. I've got my cell, though. And thanks, Rick."

"By the way, pardner, you haven't been to the Edgewater place recently, have you?"

I gulped and slammed on the brakes just before running a red light. "Me? Why would I do that?"

"Well, someone did. They broke in by the back door and trashed the downstairs."

"Geez, Rick, I would've thought you guys would be watching the place."

"We have been, but not all the time. We needed the manpower somewhere else for a couple nights, and that's when it must have happened."

"Rick, you know damn well I wouldn't trash the place."

"Yeah, I know. Steal something maybe, but not trash it. Actually, I was thinking more of the broken window pane."

"Sorry, but I'm too skilled and subtle for that kind of thing."

"Yeah, but remember, I've met your dates. They tell a different story."

"Hey, I like you, too. Later."

That, of course, pretty much made it a certainty that I would drive by the Burkhardt place to check out the damage myself. I never doubted that there was a reason Jamieson had alerted me to the break in. So I figured I'd better go see what it was.

He was right. The same small windowpane was still broken, although someone had covered the hole with duct tape. It didn't take much effort to peel the corner back, however, and unlock the door again. Jamieson had chosen a one-word description of what had happened pretty accurately. Someone had "trashed" it, smashing two of the chairs, the television set, while also dumping most of the books on the floor. What he hadn't relayed was that they had done much the same in the bedrooms upstairs. They had sliced open the mattresses and dumped the contents of the dressers and closets on the floor.

My very first thought was to check on the attic. I pushed the same dresser as before into the hallway, a much easier task this time since someone had been nice enough to remove all the drawers already. I climbed the stairs and strode over the floor beams straight to the letter boxes. Thankfully, whoever had been here since my last visit had missed the attic.

"I thought I'd find you here."

As I suspected, Jamieson had followed his hunch. He knew I wouldn't be able to resist taking a look for myself. His head peeked over the rim of the opening in the floor.

"Didn't Sherlock Holmes play a similar trick on Irene Adler?" I asked.

"If you say so. I never was the reader in our class. And I especially hate that detective shit."

"That particular 'detective shit,' as you call it, happens to be great literature. Grab a towel from the bathroom below, and I'll show you something."

Jamieson joined me a few minutes later, tossing a fresh towel in my lap. "So what's up?"

"This." I ripped off the wrapping tape and held the lid back. "You might want to haul these in for evidence at some point. They document a longstanding relationship between the Burkhardt and Harbour families. And they also suggest those notebooks we have are useless bullshit."

"So your Ray Burkhardt was trying to pull a fast one? Why?"

"Oh, he may well have believed them. I think his

granddaddy wrote them to cover his tracks. These letters point to old man Burkhardt as the real culprit behind the Peter and Paul fire."

"Then why'd he shoot Harbour?"

"I think it was kill or be killed."

"Come again?"

"The money in the Burkhardt family came from land speculation, not any bundle of cash. Apparently, the old codger turned Harbour in to the feds as a gunman and rum-runner for the mob. His payback was the opportunity to purchase the land when the feds confiscated it."

"What land was this?"

"The stuff that's been overdeveloped in northwest Indiana just south of the Indiana Tollroad. It's as bad as here. Burkhardt probably parceled it out to developers over the decades."

"How'd he know about Harbour's ill-gotten gains?"

"Well, it seems he dabbled in the profession himself. But he never got as close to the big boys as Harbour did. Old Carl even owned land and a mansion with the other mobsters at Clear Lake."

"So what did young Charlie think he was gonna do?"

"Good question. Revenge, I guess. Or blackmail. I guess that's probably what did Ray Burkhardt in after all." Jamieson paused to stare at the shards of pink insulation stuffed between the floor beams. Finally, he spoke. "I still don't get it."

"What's that?"

"What's all this got to do with the Peter and Paul fire?"

"I think that was Harbour's leverage. He was supposed to help Burkhardt. But he must have backed off, probably out of fear of pissing off his mob buddies."

"So that was more leverage Harbour had over Burkhardt, who had yet another reason to kill him." He paused. "But did he get the property before or after the killing?"

"Good question. According to the tax records I saw, the

transfer of the land happened after the fire."

"Then how did Jakob Burkhardt pull it off?"

"Easy. You pass off the shooting as a gangland hit, then say, 'Oh, by the way, his landholdings come from ill-gotten gains. And here's some proof I happened to come by.' Then you help the feds trace the money."

"You sure?"

"Not really. But it fits what I've seen so far."

Jamieson ran the towel over his face and around his neck. I did the same. When a squirrel scampered across the shingles, we both looked up at the roof.

"Jesus, it's hot up here. Let's go downstairs where I can call this in."

Moments later we sat in the kitchen. Jamieson surveyed the damage in the living room. "Any idea who did this? Local kids maybe?"

I shook my head. "I'm not so sure. I think someone -- Charlie, probably-- is getting desperate."

"He did this?"

I shook my head. "I doubt it. He can't cover that much ground, and he would've taken an awful chance coming here."

"Then who?"

"He's got friends."

"Okay, but desperate over what?"

"The secret behind this mess. He's looking for a brass ring. But I'm not sure one exists anymore that he can use. I think over the years the desire for revenge and the loss his family suffered has blurred things in his mind. I doubt he even knows what he's looking for in this magical briefcase." I studied Jamieson for a moment, trying to decide how much to tell him. "Any word on Peterson's family history?"

He let loose a light laugh. "Yeah, small world, too. Turn's out his family's from Aurora. The chief was even born there, back in '45."

My heart sank. I massaged my forehead, still wet with drops of sweat. "Oh shit, Rick."

"What now?"

"I'm not really sure. But this could go deeper than I ever realized. And even more people are in danger."

"Sheila?"

I nodded. "For one."

"How so?"

So I told him about our former KKK man over in Aurora and my appointment that evening. "That's why I think Harbour's buddies were here earlier. He probably delivered his ultimatum after they failed to turn anything up here."

"Well, you ain't goin' alone, pardner. No way."

"Rick, I don't want to bring any more danger to Sheila than she's already in."

"You still don't think she was involved in Burkhardt's death?"

"No, Rick, I don't. Not unless you can put her in that car. There are plenty of explanations for the use of that Explorer."

Jamieson stood up and stared right through me the way the nuns at Saints Peter and Paul could do. It was how they looked when they had their minds focused on some greater mission than my penmanship or misbehavior. "One of us there," Jamieson said, "will need to be thinking with his head."

I felt just as helpless sitting there as I did way back in grade school.

On the way home, the call from Charlie Harbour arrived.

"Six o'clock at the family farm, Sherlock. I want to get this thing over early."

"That's too early, asshole. I won't be there until seven." I had no real reason to insist on another hour. It wasn't like I needed the extra time to put my master plan in motion. But I wanted to challenge Harbour's sense of control.

"Sorry, Billy-boy. But you don't call the shots. Six or Sheila dies."

"Listen, asshole, you want the briefcase or not? I can't retrieve it and be there in time. I've only just located it." Another lie, of course.

"Alright, you can have your extra hour. But remember, no tricks. You know I'm serious. You want some more testimony from Sheila?"

"Leave her alone, Harbour. I know you're serious. I am, too."

I broke the connection, then drove to Staples to buy the oldest looking briefcase I could find. Then I figured I would drive over it a few times in the parking lot before heading off for Indiana.

CHAPTER SIXTEEN

In the end I left early, as though I hadn't won the delay from Harbour. I really didn't want to put my good friend Rick Jamieson on the spot. He wasn't right about which body parts were doing the thinking either.

The second call from Harbour came as I approached the state line on Route 114 just east of Kankakee. I probably added an hour to my drive, but I wanted to detour far enough south to outflank any welcoming committee that might await me. Harbout told me that instead of driving to the family farm I should continue only as far as Clear Lake, where someone would meet me at the parking lot.

I set the phone on the seat and glanced over at the battered attache case I had found in the dumpster at Staples. The lock was broken, completely jammed shut, and I never did figure out how to open the thing. But the weight felt about right. I thought that in the end this might actually buy me some time in case I needed to do something drastic, or seize an opening if one presented itself. Other than that, I didn't really have a plan to speak of.

I can't say that I was shocked to see John Wells waiting for me at Clear Lake. I had figured him for some role in this thing, however unwilling, ever since that pleasant little visit to the trailer park.

"Just what is your part in this?" I asked as I climbed from the Cabrio.

"You'll see when you get there." He nodded toward his Impala. "Get in."

I shook my head. "I don't think so. I'll keep my own wheels." I did not take it as a good sign that they wanted me to leave my car somewhere else.

"Get the fuck in, punk."

Those words came from the fat creep from my visit to

the trailer. He strolled from the shadow of a poplar tree at the edge of the lot. It was a big tree. He also had a big gun, a Magnum .357, to match his belly.

"I'm beginning to have my doubts about Hoosier hospitality, especially when unbathed slobs are involved."

The creep marched up to me, stood still for a second, then swept his hand in a wide arc toward my head. It was too wide, though, and too slow. I stepped inside it and buried my fist in his stomach. He blew a lungful of stench at my face, and I had to back up with my left hand holding on to the wrist with the weapon. I cocked my right for a knockout blow when I took one of the same just behind my right ear. A gruff 'thanks' floated above my head as I fell to the feet of John Wells. I remember wondering if everyone in Indiana wore basketball shoes on a summer night. His were Converse.

I awoke in yet another farmhouse. At least it looked like one from the vantage point of the musty sofa on which I reclined. Smelled like one, too, from the scent of manure wafting in from the neighboring fields, which was partially obscured by the smell of untreated mildew that seemed to have seeped in and spread through the walls over the years. It's probably why the wallpaper was stained varying shades of brown. Someone was holding a washcloth full of ice cubes to my forehead, while another ice pack propped up the back of my skull where John Wells had clubbed me. Once my eyes focused, I saw that the hand holding the washcloth belonged to Sheila Harbour. At least she was still alive. She gave me a smile. But it was a worrisome one, not the kind to excite confidence, much less lust. I noticed she had her jeans back on, along with a hooded University of Indiana sweatshirt. It felt kind of hot for that sort of garment, but then I had only just arrived. I worked feverishly to gather my wits, but it hurt like hell to use my head. So I put my hand over Sheila's, pressed down, then closed my eyes again.

"The Ray Burkhardt killing. Tell me it wasn't you, sweetheart."

"No," she whispered. "It was Bert. I found out the next day that he had taken my car to cover his own tracks and as a way to keep me quiet."

"You should've said something."

"Like what?"

"I'll figure it out later." I grinned and squeezed her hand. I was going to enjoy giving this to Hardy.

"Get the fuck up," Fatso barked.

"Is that all you know how to say?" I asked. "Every time your mouth opens the F-word pops out."

Sheila flipped her hand over and squeezed mine.

"Oh, cut the sweet shit, you two."

My eyes popped all the way open, surprised at the sound of Alison Peterson's voice. "What are you doing here?"

At first I was baffled by the new twist, but then I recalled what John Wells had said about her past liaisons with the likes of Charlie Harbour. I pulled myself into a sitting position, trying to hold both ice packs in place. John Wells stood off to the side shaking his head, but with his eyes fixed on the floor. Then it was clear to me why he was there.

"So it's true. She was the reason all along, wasn't she?" I shouted. "So what happens now to your real family? You just going to walk away from them?"

He didn't answer. He didn't even look at me. He had never gotten over Alison. I couldn't be sure if it was love or a lingering sense of responsibility, the kind a parent would feel toward a child, but I hoped it would give me something with which I could work if it became necessary. I figured he had to be pretty conflicted right now.

"I'll bet she never shook her granddad's influence," I went on. "Isn't it great how an abiding hatred can run from one generation to the next, destroying a person's outlook and those that come after him?"

"That's enough of the sermonizing, Billy-boy." Charlie Harbour sauntered over from his spot by the far wall to the couch. "Open this thing. And tell me where you found it." He held up the briefcase in his right hand for me to see. Then he tossed it in my lap. "How'd you seal it? Super glue?"

I picked it up and examined the lock. There were plenty of new scratches, suggesting Charlie and his crew had been trying. I wondered what we'd find inside. I tossed it aside.

"You open it. You're the one who wanted it. Just toss me some car keys, and Sheila and I will be on our way."

"Not so fast, Sherlock. Let's make sure it's the real stuff."

"Hell, Charlie, let's let 'em both have it now," Alison said. "We got what we need. With that money we can blow this place. It'll be like old times."

Well, I thought that might give me even more to work with, if she and Charlie Harbour had been an item. Charlie Harbour's smile dripped with condescension when he glanced across to the armchair in which she sat, one leg crossed over the other, ankle to knee. I doubted she noticed, though. She wore a tan windbreaker on over a light blue polo shirt and waved a hand in my direction, as though she could dismiss my presence like an ill breeze.

Harbour shook his head. "Patience, dear, patience. Let's see what we got here first. We may still need him."

"Dammit, Charlie, you're just wasting time," Alison shot back.

He took a couple steps toward her, his arm thrusting out in accusation. "Dammit yourself, Alison. If you hadn't been all fired up and in such a damn hurry, we would've been able to work Ray Burkhardt for this stuff. But now he's dead, thanks to you. And we wouldn't have the police to worry about. That one's on you, too." He shook his head. "I can't believe you were able to sucker Bert into such a stupid move.

I doubt we're going to be able to fool your uncle forever."

He turned back to me. "Now tell me where you found it and tell me just what you've got here."

I shrugged and let the ice packs drop. "I haven't the faintest idea. I haven't opened it."

"Why not?" This came from Fatso.

"Because I don't give a shit, you fat prick."

He clenched his fists, and his jaw set. I was really hoping to set something off. I figured it was probably my one chance, although now I knew I'd have to keep an eye on Alison, since she apparently had a killer's heart as well. Charlie's comment suggested she was responsible for Ray Burkhardt's death, and she appeared to act more from blood lust and impatience than calculation.

I turned my attention back to the slob. "Why don't you give Charlie's ass another kiss, and then go out and wash a tractor or something?" I added, just for fun.

He took a step forward, but Harbour put out a hand to hold him back. "I'll ask again. Where did you find it?"

"Out by Starved Rock, where it was supposed to be. I found the coordinates at Burkhardt's house before you clowns did." I nodded at Alison. "You might have gotten them yourselves if Suzy Danger over there hadn't shot Ray out of spite."

"Where?"

"In the attic. You afraid of heights, or didn't you think to look there?"

"Very clever, Sherlock. Now open it."

I picked it up. "First tell me what I'm supposed to find in here. I want to know if all this effort has been worth it."

Harbour shifted the condescending smile from Alison Peterson to me. "Well, it won't be money."

"What the…?" Alison burst out. The Fat Guy didn't look too happy either. John Wells just shook his head twice, his gaze still fixed on the floor. Then he snorted.

Harbour looked around. "Relax, everyone. The money from the investments and stocks in there will more than make up for it."

"Stocks?" I shouted. The stupefaction was hard to hide, even if I only spoke one word.

Harbour let loose a big, fat belly laugh. It was the first time I had seen his emotions go beyond one of those damn smiles. "Well, you didn't really believe that bullshit about the land, did you?"

I looked at Sheila, who sat on the arm of the sofa next to me. Her expression was as incredulous as mine probably was. At least, I think my mouth was as open as hers. "Charlie?" was all she could say.

"Oh, shit, Sheila," he said, "we were never going to rectify that. Even though he cheated our family, there was no way we could revoke that land confiscation and sale to Burkhardt. It was perfectly legal. Unfortunately."

"But then why…?"

"Granddad told me about the Ford and GE stocks ol' Carl had purchased with some of his mob money. That's what was in the briefcase when he was shot. He had just had Burkhardt purchase them in Chicago to help launder the funds and rode out on the train to meet that bastard and tell him to forget about the church. Only he discovered that that fucking pyromaniac Burkhardt had already set the fire. That's when he got shot. That stuff about a payoff was just some crap Burkhardt made up." He turned to me. "So take that, mackerel snapper."

"But how did you ever know where to find them, or who had been keeping track of them for so long?"

He turned toward Sheila. "That's where family comes in, Habermann. Sheila can read, too. And she knows how to use a library. She found out all about Peterson's background and put two and two together."

"So she's good at math. How did she know to look

into Peterson's background?" Then it hit me. I looked at Alison.

"Bingo," Harbour said.

That's when I turned to Sheila. "You broke my heart, lamb chops. Why didn't you say anything?"

I could have sworn there was water around those eyes, which made them shine like jewelry. "I'm so sorry, Bill. I didn't want you to get hurt."

"So you seduced me instead." I glanced down. "I'm a big boy. I guess I have no one to blame but myself." I looked at no one in particular. "Still, it does feel like shit." Then it hit me. "Why did you all need to go through all this crap if you had access to the briefcase through Peterson?"

Harbour studied his sister. "Sheila said Peterson no longer had the location for the stuff. Said he had lost it over the years. Good riddance to the blood money, as he called it." He shrugged. "So open it already."

I stood up at the end of this speech to position myself better. I figured Charlie was the one I needed to take care of first. What amazed me was that even though they were all armed, no one had their weapon out. Either they were afraid the neighbors might hear a shot, or they were confident they had enough strength in their numbers.

"Okay," I said. But instead I swung out and up with the hard edge of the case at his throat. "Open it yourself."

Harbour had let his arrogance get the better of him. The corner of the case caught him in the throat at the Adam's apple before he could react. He fell to his knees, both hands at his neck, gasping for air and coughing at the same time.

"You son-of-a-bitch!" It was Fatso. And his body followed those words with one, big clumsy leap. I guess he intended to hit my chest or back with a flying tackle, when he should have simply pulled his gun. But he probably wanted to get his hands on me for hurting his hero. I stepped back, and he hit the chair where Alison sat, bounced back, then took the heel of my hand in his nose. He let out a yelp as blood squirted between his fingers and down his shirt front. I walked over and kicked him in the kidneys, and he crumbled into a big ball on the floor.

Charlie Harbour had recovered enough to throw his arms around my knees, but I hammered on the back of his neck with both hands clenched together. After the third blow he let go and fell to the floor. I gave him a kick in the ribs, too. Payback may not be the charitable thing to do, but I was pretty pissed at this point.

"Bill, look out!" I swung around to see Sheila standing at the side of the sofa, pointing at Alison Peterson and John Wells. Both had Glock semi-automatics drawn and aimed at me. Wells looked stunned, his eyes finally off the floor. Alison, on the other hand, appeared to be enjoying all the commotion. They made a lovely couple. I was thrilled to see that the Sheila Harbour I remembered from our night together had come back, and that her loyalties were not as confused and uncertain as she had led on. Lord knew, I really needed her help at this point.

"Forget it," I said. "There's nothing in the case. I pulled it from a dumpster."

"Then I guess you'll have to die," Alison announced. "Just like that worthless shit Burkhardt."

"No, he won't, Alison." That sentence was spoken with a courage and firmness I did not think John Wells possessed. His weapon had also shifted in her direction.

"Yes, he will, damn you. It has to be this way." She swiveled her gun at Wells.

"Stop it, Alison. I don't want to hurt you."

"You won't, son." It was Chief Peterson.

CHAPTER SEVENTEEN

Nobody moved. Everyone just stood there as Peterson walked through the dining room. He must have entered through a back door that led to the kitchen, because I sure as hell didn't see or hear anything. He had his service revolver trained on Wells, while John kept his Glock aimed at Alison. She, in turn, had her gun leveled at me. It seemed I was the only one in the room without a weapon, and it felt very lonely.

I glanced over at Sheila, who had moved about several feet away from the sofa and toward the center of the room along the wall. Those black eyes looked as deep and as unfathomable as a coal pit. She held her hands at her sides in a pose of helplessness.

Her brother Charlie issued a low gurgling sound, followed by a groan. Peterson tossed him a quick look, then reached around his back and tossed me a pair of handcuffs. "Slap these on that son-of-a-bitch," he ordered. I obeyed.

Then Peterson turned to Wells. "Lower the gun real slow, John."

Despite the Chief's recent behavior and murky family history, I was ready to praise the Lord right then and there for his arrival. But I thought I should also remind him that Alison still had her Glock pointing straight at my stomach. She also had this sick, lost grin that spread her lips and put a shine in her eyes. I had seen something similar that first day outside the Starbuck's when Mullet-head scampered away from my car. This grimace was a lot more intense, though. I didn't like it. She didn't have a gun then either.

"Thank God you made it, Chief," I said. "But could you...?" I nodded my head in Alison's direction.

"In a minute, son," he replied. Peterson did not take his eyes off Wells. Or his gun.

Sweat dripped off an eyelash onto my shirt front. My underarms felt sticky, too.

"Not this time, Albert," Wells murmured.

It was the first time I had heard the chief's given name. More sweat.

"Just what do you think you can accomplish here, John? Why not just go on home to your wife and kids? Or are you tired of them, too?"

"Hey," I interrupted. "There's a little matter of assault and kidnapping," I reminded everyone.

Peterson cracked a smile that looked an awful lot like Alison's. "We'll see to that, son. Eventually. First, though, we have to sort this mess out."

"How'd you find us?" I asked.

"John here was not a hard one to follow, although I'd rather do it with my lights on this time of night. I waited for a bit outside to see how much more I could hear. Then you took matters into your own hands, and I knew I'd better step in before someone really got hurt."

"Well, I got impatient. It's a problem I have."

"Whatever you say." His eyes stayed with Wells the entire time. "John, what do you say?"

"I'm taking Alison with me, Chief," Wells muttered. "It's time this nonsense came to an end."

"And how do you plan to do that?"

"By taking her hand and leading her away."

"You've tried that already, and it's never worked. You just leave cleanin' this mess up to me."

Wells shook his head. Alison's tongue worked her lips, while she rubbed her free hand up and down the side of her jeans.

Then the unexpected happened. I, and apparently everyone else in the room, had forgotten about Fatso. But I guess his nose had stopped bleeding and his side had stopped aching while he worked up the courage for one last charge.

His shoulder drove my butt up toward my spine while his arms encircled my waist. Together we tumbled into the chief. A yell of pain brought everyone's attention to the center of the room where we danced a three-man two-step. Fatso's free hand waved his Magnum in the air. That was his biggest mistake.

Peterson's revolver exploded with a burst of flame and cordite that dropped Tubbo onto the carpet in a pile. Almost simultaneously Alison's Glock spat out two shots, and John Wells slid to the floor, leaving a blotch of red on the faded wallpaper behind him.

"Goddammit, Alison," Peterson yelled. "What in the hell did you do that for?"

"Goddammit yourself, Uncle Al. I wasn't going with that bastard again."

"You know damn well I'd take care of things. Haven't I always?"

Charlie Harbour lay on the floor, his eyes wide in horror. I also noticed he had wet himself. Peterson stormed over to Alison and ripped the gun from her hand. He looked to the ceiling, seemed to mutter a prayer, then reached out and pulled Alison to him.

"It'll be all right." A beefy forearm circled her neck, and she responded by embracing him at the waist. He spoke softly, as though he hoped to soothe her with his words. "I'll take care of things again. Don't worry. We'll clean this up together."

Chief Peterson turned in my direction. His revolver turned with him, and I knew all of a sudden what he meant by those reassuring words to his niece. If I'd had any water left I'd have joined Charlie Harbour.

"What's this all about, Chief?" I asked.

Peterson's eyes narrowed as he considered me. "You have any family still alive, son?"

"Yeah. Two parents and a brother down in Florida."

"Do they depend on you?"

"Not really. They're well enough off. They would miss me, though."

"Do they need you to survive in a hostile world, one that doesn't understand them?"

"You're losing me, Chief."

"Well, if they did, then maybe you'd understand what I have to do here. Family means everything, son. It's amazing what you can do when you have to protect them."

"Not to mention preserving the superiority of the white race," I said. "I know about your family."

Peterson scowled. "My grandfather was an idiot. Nobody in their right mind would believe that crap."

I nodded at Alison. "She does."

"I'm workin' on it. She needs my help, son." He studied Alison's Glock, then tossed it at my feet. "Pick it up."

"And then what?"

"And then I'll have to shoot you. Maybe you threatened me, or maybe it was accidental. I'm not sure just yet. But either way, I had to shoot you. You don't carry unauthorized firearms in the presence of a law officer. You should know that."

"Suit yourself, but Jamieson will be along any minute. He knows that this whole set-up would be a crock."

"Dream on, son. I gave that yahoo some wild-ass directions tonight. He's probably in Michigan by now."

"Fuck you, Chief. If you want to kill me, you'll have to do it in cold blood, with no evidence to support your bullshit."

"Oh, I can take care of that."

"No, you can't." It was Sheila. She had moved with the grace and speed of the first night we had met. She held Wells's weapon, and it was pointed at Peterson's back. "You're not getting away with it. Not this time."

"This time?" I repeated.

But there wasn't enough time for an answer. Alison shot across the room at Sheila, who wheeled and fired. Alison got this sudden look of surprise, awe almost, on her face. It was as though she had convinced herself that her uncle's protection had made her invincible. She stumbled backwards into her uncle, who caught her in his arms.

Peterson looked at Sheila Harbour with pure hatred etched in deep lines across his face. "You goddamn bitch." He raised his revolver.

"Don't, Chief." I pushed Alison's nice little import against his ear. "I will shoot. I can always arrange the evidence later, just like you. There's a convenient scapegoat on the floor over there." I pointed with my free hand at Harbour.

Peterson stood with his eyes locked on his niece, tears making a small, slow river down the right side of his face. Then he dropped his pistol without a word. Moving ever so slowly, he gathered Alison in his arms, walked over and laid her on the sofa.

Only then did he speak. "Okay, okay. Just call an ambulance." Tears welled in his eyes. "And hurry, please."

I looked at Sheila, whose eyes had grown wider and lighter than I had ever seen.

"You'd better call 911."

But those words did not come from Alison, or the chief, or anyone else in the room. The screen door screeched open and shut. Rick Jamieson marched into the room, his weapon drawn.

Sheila nodded and stepped toward the telephone. I moved in Jamieson's direction, my hand out to welcome someone I could finally trust. After Sheila, of course.

"I am sure glad to see you. How'd you find the place?"

"It wasn't easy. I lost the chief there on the back roads, but fortunately I heard the gunfire." He surveyed the room. "Man, you sure made a mess here. Is this Harbour?" He stepped toward Charlie's huddled form in the corner.

It was all Peterson needed. He lunged across the floor and grabbed his revolver. Jamieson saw him move before I did and plunged after him. By then Peterson had the gun in his mouth. The sound of the shot merged with Jamieson's scream for him to stop. The back of Peterson's skull exploded, spraying poor Charlie with blood and brain matter. I finally felt sorry for the bastard.

I walked straight outside and tossed my cookies over the porch railing and into a planting of small evergreens. A full moon threw shards of light through a birch tree in the front yard, and a brisk wind rustled the leaves and my hair. I thought that maybe that was the chill that had convinced Sheila to wear her sweatshirt tonight. But then I doubted that.

CHAPTER EIGHTEEN

Alison Peterson lived. She was also sentenced to 20 years for manslaughter. Sheila Harbour got probation for obstruction once she turned state's evidence against her brother. It was sweet payback for his claim that her betrayal had broken their family bond when she turned from him to me. She told me this later. He got life.

I returned to Naperville, of course, but made numerous trips back to Indiana to testify. Every once in a while Jamieson came, too, mostly as a source of moral support. But he had to testify once as well.

Sheila was there often. We acknowledged each other but never said more than a few words to one another. Social pleasantries mostly. My lawyer told me to keep my distance, and I figured her lawyer was telling her the same thing. It hurt, but I did as he said. Except for one time, when we allowed ourselves a quick hug. It still felt great, and our fingers lingered in a grasp that slipped apart as slowly as we could manage. It was then that Sheila poked a note in my pocket, which I let sit in its envelope on my desk at home for several weeks, afraid to open what I feared was a "Dear John" letter.

Everything came to a close in Starved Rock State Park, back where it started. When I finally worked up the courage to open Sheila's note, I was stunned. It contained some numbers that looked like coordinates on a map and one short sentence. "You probably want to check these out." And she had signed it, "Love, S."

I'm not much of a navigator, although I do all right with a road atlas. But I was able to mark the coordinates on a map I xeroxed at Nichols Library, then drove out west to the Park. It was a day warmed with a bright July sun, and the Park was filled with families enjoying summer in Illinois. I stood and stared at the circle I had marked on the map, which I presumed was the spot that marked the buried treasure of old stocks and bonds. I had called Sheila the night before, and she told me she had once gotten the coordinates from Peterson, who had gotten them from his father after she had told him of her research into his family's past and filled in the gaps with some educated guesses.

I asked why she hadn't passed them to her brother or checked them herself. She claimed she had been having doubts about Charlie and the whole affair for some time. That's why Bert the Mullet-Man had used her car. He had noticed the change and wanted to lock her in. I also asked if Peterson had ever checked the spot out. "Yeah, probably. You'll see why he did what he did soon enough."

Glancing at the map, I figured this may have been what Ray Burkhardt had had in mind the night we met. Only Sheila Harbour had beaten him to it. She had blackmailed Peterson, threatening exposure for his protection of Alison over the years, behavior that had culminated in the death of Ray Burkhardt. She also told me I'd be disappointed in what I found and that she was glad now to be rid of the entire business.

A hand brushed the hair at the back of my head, just like that day in Peterson's office. I turned slowly, afraid I might scare the moment away. Sheila stood just inches behind me. She had snuck up on my once more, and I swore it would be the last time.

"Howdy, beautiful. What brings you here?" I inquired.

I took in those long, lovely legs hiding in a pair of black calf-length slacks that fit her shape like a soft sculpture, her upper body resting under a white cotton tank top and the long, dark tresses that ran past golden brown shoulders.

"Just out for a drive on a beautiful day," she replied.

I took her hand and gazed into those eyes for what seemed like days. Whole childhoods passed. It was just long enough, I thought, to make up for the time lost since that night in Indiana.

"You hungry? I'd love to buy you lunch. Dinner, too. And then breakfast."

She smiled. The best one yet. She leaned in close and brushed my lips with hers, circled my neck with her arms, then let her mouth rest on mine for the moment.

"Let's go," she said, finally.

We walked to my car. Only then did I see Jamieson's Thunderbird on its way out past the Park entrance. I turned for a last look at the spot marked by an X. On top of it sat tons of rock, concrete, glass, steel and timber. Someone had built a lodge over a fortune. I couldn't have cared less.

CPSIA information can be obtained at www.ICGtesting.com
265426BV00001B/2/P